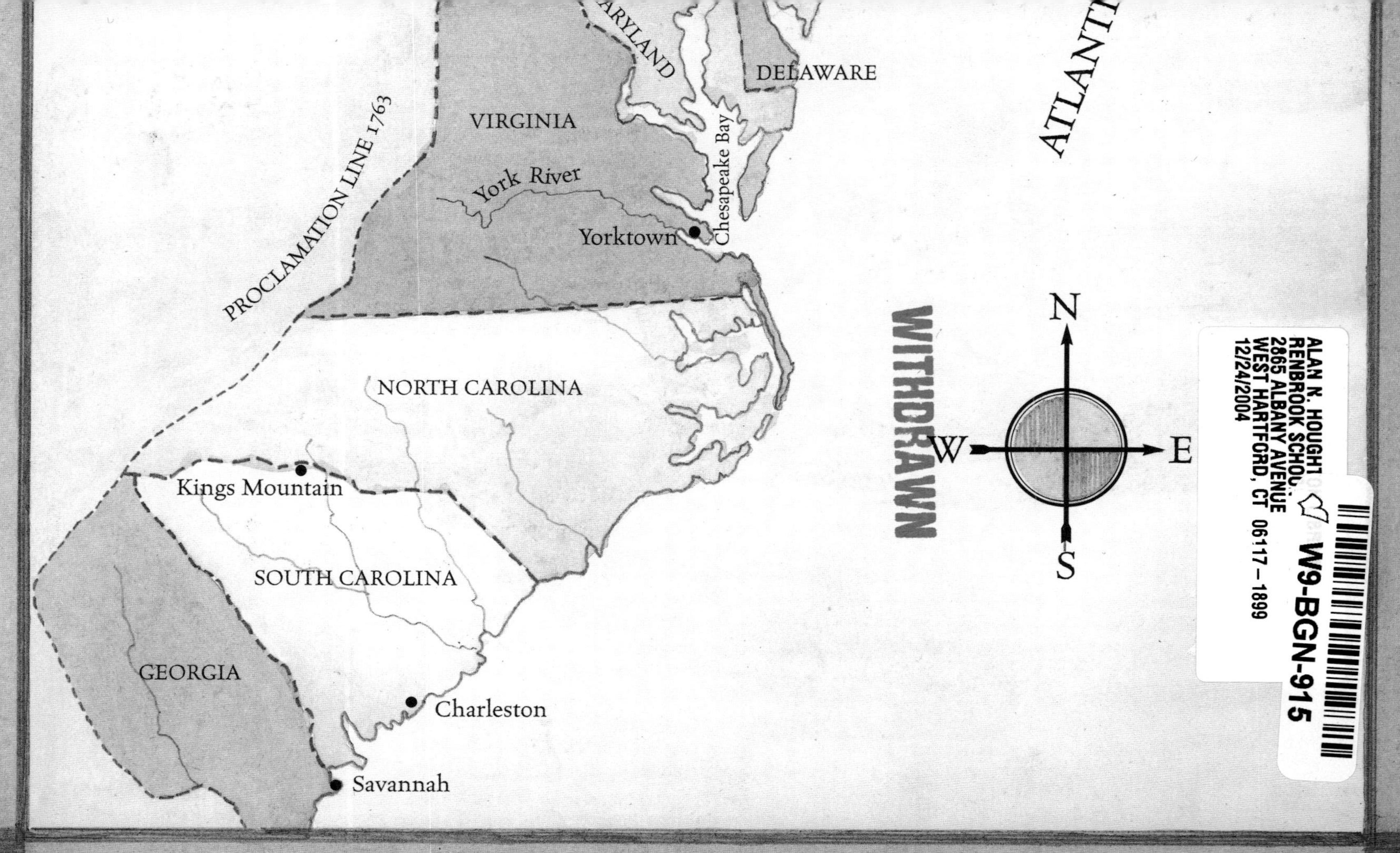
ARYLAND
DELAWARE
ATLANTI
VIRGINIA
PROCLAMATION LINE 1763
York River
Chesapeake Bay
Yorktown
N
W
E
S
NORTH CAROLINA
Kings Mountain
SOUTH CAROLINA
GEORGIA
Charleston
Savannah

YOUNG PATRIOTS

YOUNG PATRIOTS

Inspiring Stories of the American Revolution

by Marcella Fisher Anderson and Elizabeth Weiss Vollstadt

Boyds Mills Press

Many thanks to Molly Perry for contributing her story "A Seder Night in Charleston."

Many thanks to Karie Diethorn, chief curator, Independence National Historical Park, for her help with the illustrations.

Published by Boyds Mills Press, Inc.
A Highlights Company
815 Church Street
Honesdale, Pennsylvania 18431
Printed in China

Publisher Cataloging-in-Publication Data (U.S.)

Anderson, Marcella Fisher.
Young patriots: inspiring stories of the American Revolution / by Marcella Fisher Anderson and Elizabeth Weiss Vollstadt.—1st ed.
[143] p. : ill. ; cm.
Includes bibliographical references.
Summary: Fifteen stories describing the experiences of young people during critical moments of the American Revolution, including the battles in New York, Saratoga, Trenton and Valley Forge, and events of the Boston Tea Party, Paul Revere's Ride, the Constitutional Convention and others.
ISBN 1-59078-241-0
1. United States—History — Revolution, 1775–1783—Juvenile fiction. 2. United States—History—Revolution, 1775–1783—Anecdotes—Juvenile fiction. (1. United States—History—Revolution, 1775–1783—Fiction.) I. Vollstadt, Elizabeth Weiss, 1942– II. Title
[F] 22 PZ7.A54397Yo 2004
2003115295

First edition, 2004
The text of this book is set in 13-point Minion.

10 9 8 7 6 5 4 3 2 1

To my husband, Glenn, for showing patience during the times I "lived" in Revolutionary War America; for searching out the most knowledgeable person at historic sites; and for sharing in the enthusiasm, this book is lovingly dedicated.

—M. F. A.

To my husband, Peter, for his support and encouragement as I spent countless hours at the computer; and for his willingness to traipse around numerous historic sites with me, this book is dedicated with love.

—E. W. V.

CONTENTS

Foreword ix
Acknowledgments xi
Introduction xiii

I. THE ROAD TO WAR

December 1773 ~ Polly and the Boston Tea Party 4
Polly is a fictional girl in colonial Boston who hides important papers from the British and earns her father's respect.

January 1775 ~ Soldiers, Sleds, and Sam 11
A boy and his friends confront a British general about his servant ruining their favorite sledding hill. The story is based on a true incident described in a letter from a Boston man.

March 1775 ~ Stopped by a Shadow 17
Seen through the eyes of a free black servant girl, this story is based on a historical possibility that ruined British plans to seize John Hancock and Samuel Adams at a patriot gathering in Boston.

II. HOSTILITIES BEGIN

April 18, 1775 ~ Nothing Stops Paul Revere 26
Imagine Paul Revere forgetting his spurs on the night of April 18! This story, based on a Revere family legend, describes the last-minute delivery of Revere's spurs before his famous ride to Lexington.

April 19, 1775 ~ Just Like a Minuteman 31
Hannah Barns, a girl in Concord, Massachusetts, prevents the British from searching a trunk containing gold and important papers. The story is fiction but is based on historic accounts about the real Hannah Barns.

July 8, 1776 ~ The Day the Bell Rang 39
A boy takes part in the celebration of the signing of the Declaration of Independence.

III. THE REVOLUTION IN THE NORTH

Christmas, 1776 ~ Across the Delaware 48
A boy returning to his home on the New Jersey side of the Delaware River becomes unexpectedly involved in the crossing of Washington's army and the surprise attack on the Hessians at Trenton.

October 1777 ~ Dark Forest Danger 55
A girl returns to her home in the New York wilderness and finds herself sharing the forest with British soldiers and their Indian allies at the Battle of Saratoga.
March 1778 ~ A Soldier Is Born 65
A sixteen-year-old soldier at Valley Forge grumbles when he is mistakenly placed in a model company training under the colorful Baron von Steuben.

IV. THE REVOLUTION IN THE SOUTH

April 1780 ~ A Seder Night in Charleston 78
During the British siege of Charleston, South Carolina, young Moses Sheftall finds that he has both strength and courage. This fictional story is based on the life of the real Moses Sheftall.
Fall 1780 ~ William's War 88
A North Carolina boy longs for revenge against the Loyalists—until the enemy at Kings Mountain wears a familiar face.
October 1781 ~ Thanks Be! 98
Despite being on different sides, a colonial boy and a young British drummer become friends in the days just before British general Charles Cornwallis's surrender at Yorktown.

V. A NEW COUNTRY IS BORN

July 1782 ~ New Day in Savannah 108
With the war won by the patriots, a thirteen-year-old boy is dismayed to learn that his Loyalist father plans to take him and his brother back to England.
August 1787 ~ Constitution Summer 118
A girl will never forget how she helped keep a spy from learning secrets of the Constitutional Convention.
April 1789 ~ Learning from the President 126
A boy experiences the first presidential inauguration and discovers that George Washington is only human.
Time Line 134
Glossary 137
Further Reading 140

FOREWORD

Historians now know a great deal about the American Revolutionary era. They know about the protests that learned colonists wrote to object to British taxation and other measures. They know about the street demonstrations of common people designed not only to object to British policies but also to vent their frustrations at their colonial betters. They know about the boycotts of British goods, how they were enforced, and who obeyed or disobeyed them. They know about the politically active patriots, those men who met in colonial legislatures and in intercolonial meetings, such as the Stamp Act Congress and the Continental Congress, and almost everything they said or wrote.

Historians also know almost everything about fighting the war—what the engagements were, who fought on each side, their fighting techniques, their weapons, even the casualties they suffered. They know how the common soldiers and their officers in each army and the militia dressed, ate, marched, camped, how they felt about each other, and how orders were transmitted. They know these things about the British, French, and American forces.

In recent years, historians have come to know more about the home front during the war. They know what women experienced when their fathers, husbands, or brothers went off to fight, and what happened to them if their men did not return. They know what the marching armies or marauding naval forces did to the countryside, the occupied cities, and the raided seacoast towns. They know how the tumult caused by the war affected farming and trading, how it affected religion and education, how it affected local politics, how it affected the settlement of the frontier and the Indians who lived there (and who generally had to choose to fight either for the British or the Americans). They know how the war changed slavery, setting it on the road to extinction in the North, but not in the South.

They even know the deliberations of the Constitutional Convention, that then-secret meeting that transformed the national government, setting many of the precedents by which it operates today.

Yet one area historians know little about is what young boys and girls did during the Revolutionary era. For all these other events and groups there survives written evidence to tell us what happened and how people participated. But for young people there is very little. They, themselves, did not provide it. Some could not read or write. Most had not the time, the resources, nor the inclination to keep a diary or write letters. Their parents and other adults, preoccupied with the war and survival, rarely recorded the doings or feelings of the young.

In order to tell the stories of young people during the Revolution, the authors of this book have immersed themselves in what historians know, have relied on documents and family legends when they could, and from that knowledge have very skillfully imagined young people into many of the key incidents of the era. Through these stories—as well as the introductions, sidebars, and illustrations—young readers can learn about pre-war protests, the major events and military engagements, and the intriguing aftermath of the American Revolution. Best of all, they will experience the sensations of being, as John Adams once put it, "in the midst of a revolution the most complete, unexpected, and remarkable of any in the history of nations."*

David W. Robson
Professor of History
John Carroll University

* From a letter to William Cushing, June 9, 1776. Paul H. Smith et al., eds., *Letters of the Delegates of Congress, 1774–1789.* 26 vols. Washington, D.C.: Library of Congress, 1976–98, IV, 177.

ACKNOWLEDGMENTS

Many generous people help with the making of a book. For their interest and kind assistance, we would like to thank the following: lead consultant David W. Robson, Ph.D., John Carroll University, University Heights, Ohio, who searched out primary sources and allowed us reasonable latitude in our historical fiction while keeping us true to the facts; classroom consultant Samantha Schaedler, a National Board Certified Teacher of Social Studies, Orange Schools, Pepper Pike, Ohio, who read the entire manuscript and provided insights into student interest in particular people and events of the American Revolution.

By letter, e-mail, and telephone, we received invaluable fact checking from our experts, who willingly shared their specific knowledge with us: J. L. Bell, historical researcher, and Nancy Richard, Library Director, Bostonian Society, Boston; Joseph Lee Boyle, former Historian, Valley Forge National Historical Park, Valley Forge, Pennsylvania; Anthony Brown, Ranger, Independence National Historical Park, Philadelphia; Diane K. Depew, Supervisory Park Ranger, Colonial National Historical Park, Yorktown, Virginia; Roy Goodman, Curator of Printed Materials, American Philosophical Society Library,

Philadelphia; Timothy A. Holmes, Historian and Information Officer, Old Saratoga, New York; Sondra Leiman, former teacher and author of *America: The Jewish Experience*, Bronx, New York; Whitney Lloyd, teacher of American history, University School, Hunting Valley, Ohio; Michelle Matz, Educator, Washington Crossing Historic Park, Washington Crossing, Pennsylvania; Christopher C. Revels, Chief Ranger, Kings Mountain National Military Park, Blacksburg, South Carolina; Henry Baird Tenney, descendant of the Ottawa Nation, Cleveland Heights, Ohio; Anna Coxe Toogood, Historian and Cultural Resources Management, Independence National Historical Park, Philadelphia; Leslie Perrin Wilson, Curator of Special Collections, Concord Free Public Library, Concord, Massachusetts.

Appreciation goes to other people as well: Debra Brass, Children's Librarian, Cuyahoga County Public Library, Cleveland, for tracking down needed reference materials; Florence and Alton G. Gardner, former education professors, for giving thoughtful consideration to the book while at Chautauqua, New York; grandson Jonathan Distad and Betsy Gustafson for generously providing computer support; grandson Henry Distad and cohorts—Jacob Alaburda, Ben Newton, Alec Riffle, and Patrick Scott, Shaker Middle School students, Shaker Heights, Ohio—for reading entries and answering a questionnaire. As always, Marcella's Monday Night Writers group in Cleveland and Elizabeth's critique group in DeLand, Florida, offered clear insights and constant encouragement.

Finally, we are indebted to our editor, Carolyn P. Yoder, for her frequent reassurances of "all's well" and her ability to keep this project on track. Special thanks to our publisher, Kent L. Brown Jr.—writers for young people could have no better advocate.

Marcella Anderson
Elizabeth Vollstadt

INTRODUCTION

During the first half of the 1700s, most American colonists were proud to be British subjects. Unlike people in many other countries, British citizens had rights that not even the king could violate. For example, the king could not take a person's property without the approval of Parliament. Nor could a person be thrown into jail without being told the charges against him. Also, through representatives in Parliament, British citizens had the right to vote on taxes. American colonists took these rights for granted and were loyal to the mother country.

When Britain went to war with France over territory in America—the French and Indian War—many colonists fought alongside the British soldiers. George Washington served as an aide to British general Edward Braddock and also commanded a regiment of the Virginia militia. The British regulars, as the soldiers were called, and the American militiamen had their disagreements and often didn't like each other at all, but they stood together against their common enemies. When the war ended in 1763, however, tensions between the colonists and Britain began to grow. What caused these tensions?

One cause was the French and Indian War itself. It was very

expensive. Because the war was fought in North America, Britain believed that the American colonies should help pay for it. Britain also believed that the colonists should help pay for the troops sent to protect their western borders from the Indians.

So the British Parliament levied a series of new taxes on the colonists. The first was the Sugar Act in 1764, which taxed all sugar and molasses that came into the colonies. Molasses was imported from the West Indies and was used for the profitable business of making rum. Massachusetts and New York both protested loudly against the tax. Massachusetts said that it violated the colony's charter. The New York assembly said that there could be "no liberty, no happiness, no security" if the British Parliament could levy such a tax.

But Britain ignored these protests and passed another tax in 1765—the Stamp Act. This act made colonists buy a stamp to place on legal documents, such as wills, marriage licenses, and contracts. It also taxed newspapers, pamphlets, and even playing cards. Once again, colonists from Virginia to Massachusetts protested the tax. Some, such as Patrick Henry of Virginia, questioned Britain's right to levy such a tax. Others protested more violently. In New York and Boston, demonstrators rioted and attacked the homes and offices of stamp tax collectors.

The Stamp Act was repealed a year later in 1766, but then Parliament passed the Declaratory Act, which reasserted its right to tax the colonies whenever and however it wished. In 1767, it passed the Townshend Acts, which imposed new taxes on everyday household items such as glass, paint, paper, lead, and tea. Again the colonists protested, arguing that they were not represented in Parliament. "Taxation without representation is tyranny" became a rallying cry.

Samuel Adams of Boston wrote an open letter to all the colonies urging that they boycott British goods until the tax was repealed. Other colonists took to the streets, rioting against British officials. In Boston, some officials feared for their lives and asked the British government for protection. The government sent two thousand British troops to Boston, but they only made the situation worse, as they were a constant reminder of the colonists' complaints. Tensions continued to rise and finally exploded into battle in the Massachusetts towns of Lexington and Concord in 1775.

Once begun, the Revolutionary War was a long conflict, filled with many hardships. Young people shared in those hardships, and many did their part to help the patriot cause. Fifteen-year-old Joseph Plumb Martin of Connecticut joined the Continental army and kept a journal that is still read today. Ten-year-old Israel Task of Massachusetts served as a cook and messenger for the Continental army. Susanna Bolling of Virginia was a teenager when she left her home and rowed across the Appomattox River to warn the marquis de Lafayette and his patriot soldiers that the British were coming to capture them. African American James Forten served as a powder boy on the American ship *Royal Louis* when he was fourteen. And sixteen-year-old Thomas Young fought barefoot up Kings Mountain, South Carolina, to help the Americans win a great victory.

These are just a few of the young people whose contributions were noticed and remembered. But many others also helped the American cause. We will never know all of their names or everything they did, but it is fun and interesting to imagine the adventures they might have had. That is what the authors of this book have done. In some stories, they have taken real young people from the pages of history and imagined the details of their lives and how they might have felt as they participated in exciting events. In other stories, the authors have created fictional characters and placed them in actual historical events. All of the stories show how young people just like you helped win America's independence and witnessed the dawn of a new day of liberty.

YOUNG PATRIOTS

I

THE ROAD TO WAR

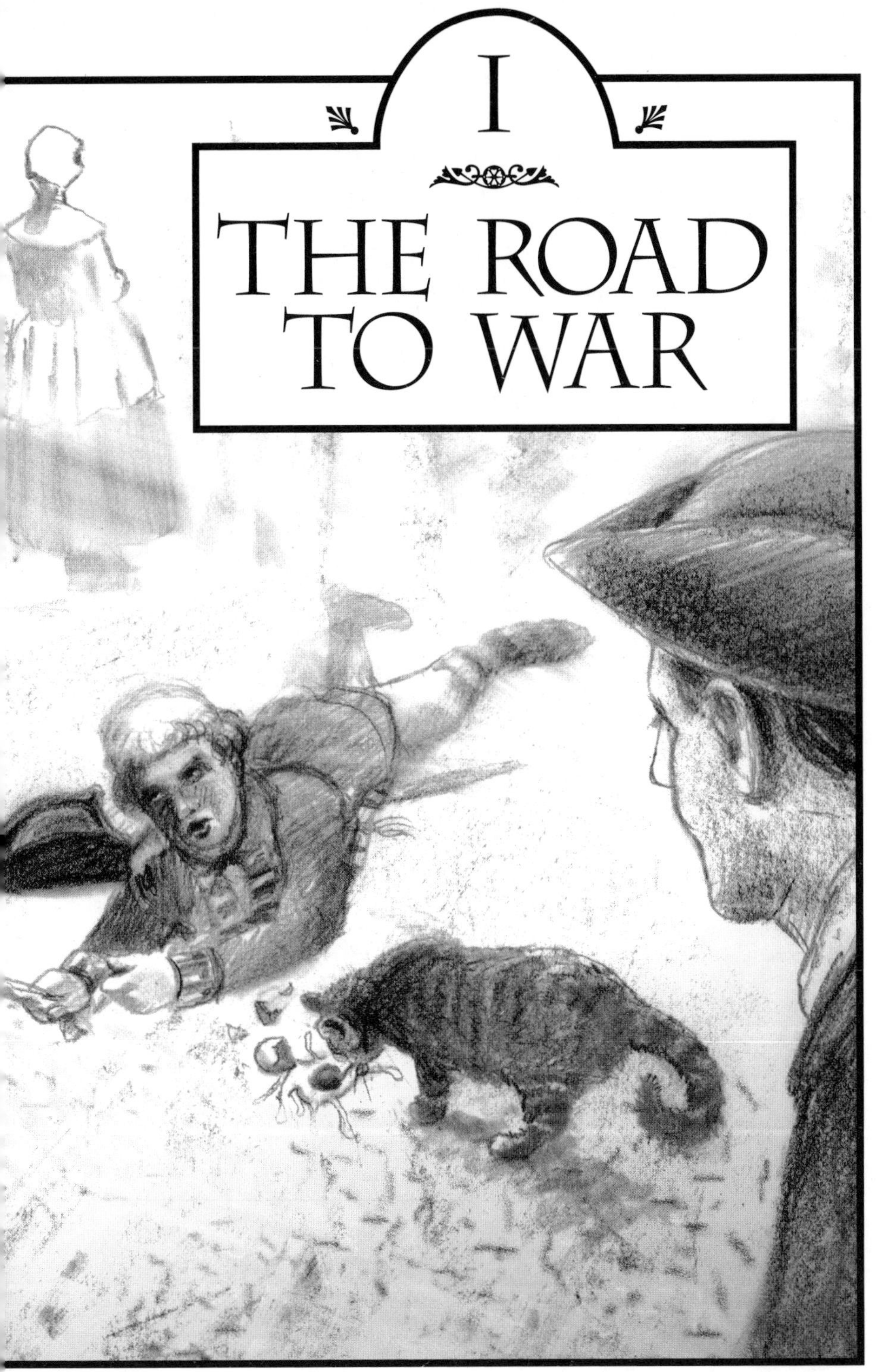

"Stopped by a Shadow" on pages 17–23

POLLY AND THE BOSTON TEA PARTY

by Elizabeth Weiss Vollstadt

As the year 1773 drew to a close, Boston patriots faced a dilemma. Although most of the taxes under the Townshend Acts had been repealed in 1770, a small tax remained on tea. For a few years, no one paid much attention, and many colonists avoided the tax altogether by purchasing tea smuggled in from Holland and the Dutch West Indies.

The British government, however, was not happy that the colonists were buying smuggled tea. The East India Company of London, which dominated Britain's tea trade, was slowly sliding into bankruptcy. To save the company, the government passed the Tea Act of 1773. The law required that the colonists buy tea only from the East India Company and only through selected merchants to ensure that the tax was paid. Opposition to the Tea Act began to mount.

In December 1773, three tea ships—the Dartmouth, Eleanor, *and* Beaver*—were docked at Griffin's Wharf in Boston. The colonists refused to let the tea be unloaded. The royal governor of Massachusetts, Thomas Hutchinson, refused to let the ships return to London. Things could have stayed that way for a long time, except that the law also said that the cargo had to be unloaded and taxes paid within twenty days. If not, the cargo could be seized by customs officials and the duties paid. The deadline was December 17. Determined to keep the tea from being unloaded, the patriots took action on the night of December 16, 1773, and held a tea party like no other.*

POLLY CHANDLER LISTENED TO HER FATHER and brother talk about the tea ships. Christmas, 1773, was almost here, but it seemed as if no one in Boston could think of anything but tea.

"I don't understand," she said. "Why can't we just pay the tax? It's really not that much."

"True enough," answered her brother, Thomas, "but it's not the amount that matters." His brown eyes opened wider as he leaned forward to explain. Thomas was fifteen, two years older than Polly, and he liked to think of himself as a man.

"You see, Polly, if we voted on the tea tax, no one would mind paying. But the king is trying to tax us without our consent. Well, we're going to teach those **redcoats** a lesson. After tonight—"

"That's enough, Thomas!" Mr. Chandler interrupted. "There's no need to start worrying your mother."

But Polly could see that it was too late. Her mother had already turned from the fire where she was ladling soup into the big serving dish.

"What *about* tonight? What's going to happen?" Mrs. Chandler asked.

With an angry look at Thomas, Mr. Chandler started to explain.

REDCOATS—*A name the colonists gave to the British regulars because of the red uniforms they wore. Another, more insulting name was lobsterbacks.*

"The governor insists that the tea be unloaded and the tax be paid. If Samuel Adams can't persuade him to change his mind, we'll have to do something. That tea must not land on American soil!"

Suddenly, there was a loud knock on the door. Before anyone could get up, it was flung open and quickly shut again. A tall man whom Polly had never seen before anxiously looked around.

"Excuse me for barging in like this," he said, with a nod at Mrs. Chandler, "but there's no time to waste."

He turned to Polly's father and pulled a bundle of papers from under his large gray overcoat.

"Samuel Adams was afraid that after tonight his house might be searched, so he asked me to find a safe place for these papers. No one knows that you and Thomas are involved with us. Can we leave them here?"

Polly saw her father hesitate. "For a short time," he finally said. "I don't want trouble for my family."

"Of course," said the stranger. "But for now, take care that they're well hidden. If these papers are found, the lives of many patriots will be in danger."

He turned to leave, then he paused. "Will we see you and Thomas at the meeting this afternoon?"

Mr. Chandler nodded, and their strange visitor opened the door. He quickly looked up and down the street before slipping out.

Polly ran to her father, almost dancing with excitement.

"Can I come with you? Please! I know that something is going to happen, and I want to be there, too."

"No," said Mr. Chandler. "A public meeting of this nature is no place for young ladies." His voice softened, and he put his arm around her. "Besides, don't you have that new dress to finish for Christmas?"

Polly glared at her sewing basket. "Who cares about an old dress? I want to go with you and Thomas."

But her father was firm. He and Thomas left without her.

"It's not fair! It's just not fair!" exclaimed Polly, kicking her sewing basket.

"Maybe it's not," her mother said kindly, "but let's do what we can to help here." She picked up the bundle of papers and looked around the room. "Now where can we put . . ."

Before she could finish, there was a heavy pounding on the door.

"Open up in the name of the king!" shouted a man's voice. "This is Captain Smith, and I have orders to search this house for evidence of treason."

Mrs. Chandler clutched the papers to herself and froze. Polly looked at her mother and knew that something had to be done. But what?

Then she noticed her sewing basket. Maybe it could be useful after all!

She ran to her mother and grabbed the bundle. "Quick, answer the door before he thinks something is wrong!"

She raced back to her sewing basket and pulled out her new green dress. Then she stuffed the papers in the basket and pushed it over to the chair by the fireplace.

By the time her mother had the door open, Polly was calmly sitting by the fire mending a pair of socks. She looked as if she had been there for hours. Her wide skirt was draped over the sewing basket, which was bursting with breeches and stockings and was topped off by her half-finished dress.

"Good afternoon," said the soldier, his red uniform announcing his importance. "We've heard that you're hiding information about those who oppose the king."

"I don't know what you're talking about," said Polly's mother. "There's no one here but my daughter and me. And we're not hiding anything."

The soldier opened cupboards, looked in the pantry, and turned over the big black pot that was sitting next to the fireplace. He even went up the wooden stairs, and Polly could hear him opening the wardrobe doors.

"Are you quite finished?" asked Mrs. Chandler when the soldier returned empty-handed. "Now will you go and leave us in peace?"

The captain looked around the room again. Then he looked hard at Polly. "Get up a minute, young lady. What might you be hiding with your long skirt?"

Polly's heart started to pound, but she stood up and even managed a smile.

"Only my sewing basket," she said. "It's full of mending. See?" She reached in and pulled out a pair of Thomas's breeches with a hole in the knee. "And here is a new dress for me. Would you like to see it?"

She started to pick up the dress, but the officer had already turned away.

"I'm sorry to have bothered you," he said to Mrs. Chandler. "Perhaps we were given the wrong information . . . this time." He bowed stiffly and left.

When she could no longer hear his footsteps on the cobblestones, Polly ran over to the door and bolted it. Then she hugged her mother, who hadn't moved.

"We did it!" she exclaimed. "We fooled the redcoat!"

A few hours later, she was hugging her father just as hard. After hearing about the afternoon's adventure, he said, "What a cool head you have, Polly! A lot of men will be very grateful to you and your sewing basket. I cannot bring you to the meeting this evening, but if events go as we fear, I will be back for you. You deserve to see what happens to the tea."

Polly's thoughts raced as she waited. What was happening at the meeting? Would her father come for her?

Finally, the door burst open. "Come quickly, Polly," her father said. "The governor has refused our plea to return the tea to England. We are taking action."

The narrow streets of Boston grew more crowded as they drew near the harbor. Polly's father pushed forward until they reached Griffin's Wharf.

"Look! Over there!" someone shouted.

Polly turned to see groups of men dressed as Indians board the tea ships.

"There's Thomas!" she said, recognizing her brother despite the Indian paint on his face.

"Shhh," cautioned her father. "No one must ever know who the 'Indians' are."

Remembering the British officer who searched their house, Polly nodded and stood quietly with the crowd as the "Indians" dumped the tea into the harbor. They worked quickly, and in a few hours the task was over.

But as she walked home between her father and brother, Polly somehow knew that this was just the beginning. And thanks to her sewing basket, she would be part of whatever followed.

Did you know . . . that during colonial times, government officials, including the occupying British troops, had the right to search people's homes at any time? This practice of "search and seizure" was so distasteful to the colonists that the Fourth Amendment to the Constitution, part of the Bill of Rights, states that no one can enter a person's home without a legal paper called a warrant.

Do you wonder . . . who the "Indians" who took part in the Boston Tea Party really were? They were young men like Polly's brother. Many were apprentices, bound out to tradesmen to work and learn their trade. They were chosen to dump the tea because they would not be recognized. Only a few patriot leaders, including Paul Revere, went along to make sure the protest didn't turn into a riot.

The Boston Tea Party

SOLDIERS, SLEDS, AND SAM

by Elizabeth Weiss Vollstadt

The British government made Boston pay a high price for destroying the tea. The busy port of Boston, on which most Bostonians depended, was closed. More troops arrived. But resistance to British rule kept growing. Many young people followed their parents' example in standing up to the British, although their concerns were not necessarily about taxation. Sometimes they were more concerned with enjoying their favorite sports and other activities. Sometimes, too, the British officers tried to be good neighbors.

One example of this "good neighbor policy" is described in a letter written on January 29, 1775, by John Andrews of Boston to his brother-in-law in Philadelphia. It tells about a group of boys who complained to British general Frederick Haldimand when his servant ruined their favorite sledding hill by spreading ashes on it. The general listened to them and ordered his servant to repair the damage.

Andrews's letter went on to say that when British general Thomas Gage, who was the governor of Massachusetts, heard about the incident, he observed that "it was impossible to beat the notion of Liberty out of the people, as it was rooted in 'em from their Childhood."

This story is based on that incident.

THE SNOW SQUEAKED BENEATH THEIR BOOTS as the three boys tramped toward Sherburn's Hill, their favorite coasting hill in all of Boston. The streets were quiet that snowy January morning in 1775. Only a tight group of British soldiers marched boldly past the silent houses.

The boys ignored the soldiers. They were used to them. A few thousand British troops were now in Boston, hoping to crush the colonists' growing rebellion against the king and his laws.

"Hurry, Sam," called Edward. "You're making us late again!"

Sam struggled to keep up with his brother and their friend Joshua. He wanted to ride the big wooden sled down Sherburn's Hill to School Street, just as they did. But his stiff right leg slowed him down.

Every step reminded Sam of that awful day last spring when a British officer had come to his father's blacksmith shop.

"Hurry," the officer ordered. "This horse needs a new shoe at once."

Sam was proud to hold the horse's leg for his father. But then the horse had kicked hard. A bone in Sam's leg cracked. The break hadn't healed properly.

Now Sam's cheeks turned red when Joshua said, "I thought we were going to get there early today—before General Haldimand's servant came out."

Sam protested, "It's not my fault the servant sprinkles ashes on our coasting hill when he cleans the general's fireplace."

But Joshua didn't hear. They were at School Street at last. Joshua looked up and groaned, "Oh, no, late again."

Sam and Edward looked, too. A man was standing in the middle of Sherburn's Hill, trampling the snow and scattering ashes.

"Well, that's it," said Edward. He kicked the sled. "If we'd gotten here sooner, we could have had a few good runs before he ruined our hill."

"Sure could have," said Joshua. He looked at Sam. "Next time *he* stays home."

Sam jammed his icy fingers into his pockets. He lifted his chin. "I may be slow," he finally said, "but I'm not afraid of the redcoats. I'll get the servant to stop."

The two older boys hooted with laughter. "You?" said Joshua. "What can you do?"

"I'll . . ." Sam hesitated. What could he do? He looked at the servant again. "I'll tell him to scatter the ashes someplace else."

"Go ahead," Edward said, "if you dare."

Sam didn't want to dare. He wanted to go home. But he was tired of the jeering remarks. He started to limp up the hill. Edward and Joshua followed. The cold wind bit into Sam's cheeks, but he kept going until he reached the servant.

"Please, sir," Sam said, "I . . . I'd like to make a request."

The man frowned. "And what might that be?"

"Could you . . . could you . . ." Sam wanted to run, but he had come too far. "Could you scatter the ashes someplace else? They ruin the snow, and we can't coast."

The servant laughed, but it wasn't a happy sound. "What do I care for your hill? I will scatter the general's ashes wherever I wish," he said. "It is not for colonist children to tell the British army what to do. Now run along before I—"

Sam didn't hear the rest. Edward grabbed his arm and pulled him away.

"Come on," he said.

Sam followed Edward and Joshua. How he despised that servant! And the general! And the whole British army! Coasting was the one time his bad leg didn't matter. He could fly down the hills as fast as anyone.

"Stop!" Sam called suddenly. "I'm going to see General Haldimand himself."

"Then you're going alone," said Joshua. "He'll never listen to us."

Edward looked at Joshua. "We'd better stay with Sam," he said. "Ma will blame me if anything happens to him."

Sam headed for the general's house. He could feel his heart—*thump . . . thump . . . thump*—like the steady beat of a drum. He stopped at the heavy wooden door. His knees shook. But he lifted his hand, made a fist, and pounded as hard as he could. A young soldier opened the door.

"Who is it, Private?" a voice boomed from inside. "Let them in and close the door! The wind will blow my fire out!"

The three boys crowded into the hall. A big man in a red uniform stood in a doorway. Joshua and Edward pushed Sam in front of them.

"I'm General Haldimand," the man said. He led them into his office. Flames leaped about in a huge stone fireplace. Sam took off his woolen hat and twisted it. The snow melted off his clothes with a steady drip. His leg felt tired and sore.

"Go on . . . you started this," Edward hissed.

Sam swallowed. "Well, sir . . . ," he began. He told the general about the hill and the servant. "We are free citizens of Boston," he said. "You have no right to destroy our hill."

General Haldimand frowned. Edward tugged at Sam's sleeve. "Let's go," he whispered.

But this time Sam stood his ground. For ten long seconds, no one moved.

Then the general raised his hands and smiled. "You win, my lad," he said. He turned to the private, who was standing in the doorway.

"These lads are surrounded by talk of liberty and rights every day of their lives," he said. "It's no wonder that they come marching to me with such demands."

He looked at Sam. "There are already bad feelings between our army and the people of Boston. I shall not add to them. I shall give orders that my servant repair the damage and no longer scatter ashes on your hill."

Back outside, Joshua and Edward whooped and shouted in the falling snow. Edward draped his arm around Sam's shoulder. Joshua patted Sam on the back. "You can have the first coast tomorrow," he said. "Even if you are the last one to reach the hill."

Sam's eyes shone. His sled would fly faster than anyone's! The boys tramped home together through the snow. And no one told Sam to hurry up—not once.

Did you know . . . that sledding, or coasting, was popular among boys in colonial times and that Sherburn's Hill in Boston was a favorite of more than a generation of boys? Colonial children played some games that children still play today—hide-and-seek, blindman's bluff, lacrosse, hopscotch, and jump rope. They also liked to fly kites. Girls played with dolls. Most dolls were homemade of wooden pegs, but many were nicely dressed. One favorite game that is no longer played was hoop and stick. The hoop was about two and a half feet across and the stick about nine inches long. Boys would run alongside the hoop, moving it along with the stick. Girls, on the other hand, would stand and use their sticks to pass the hoop back and forth from one to the other.

British troops and local boys in Boston

STOPPED BY A SHADOW

by Marcella Fisher Anderson

Although some gestures of friendship were common between the British soldiers and the colonists, relationships were always strained. On March 5, 1770, the situation led to a bloody confrontation that became known as the Boston Massacre. Determined never to forget the event, Bostonians met each year on that date at the Old South Meeting House to commemorate the massacre with lengthy, fiery speeches.

By early 1775, a group of officers on the staff of British general Thomas Gage became frustrated that Gage had not taken action to end the Bostonians' open and escalating resentment against the British soldiers who occupied their city. Gage was not only the commander of the British forces stationed in Boston but also the royal governor of Massachusetts. The former governor, Thomas Hutchinson, had been relieved of his duties and was back in England.

On numerous occasions, the colonists suspected British plots to arrest two of their leaders, John Hancock and Samuel Adams. A prosperous member of the shipping trade, Hancock was considered the wealthiest man in the colonies and a champion of the patriot cause. Samuel Adams was an organizer of the ***Sons of Liberty*** *and a tireless opponent of compromise with Britain.*

The fifth anniversary of the Boston Massacre, in 1775, fell on a Sunday. To honor the Sabbath, the commemoration was held on Monday, March 6. The event was expected to attract an especially large gathering of the Sons of Liberty. British officers reasoned that it would be a good time to seize the rebel leaders. It is thought that they ordered a young army **ensign** *to throw a raw egg at the meeting's main speaker, Dr. Joseph Warren, as a signal to arrest Adams and Hancock. However, the ensign fell and injured his knee on the way to the Old South Meeting House, and the signal was never given.*

The streets of Boston that day would have been filled with colonists hurrying to the meeting. Like the people in this story, cabinetmakers, apprentices, and kitchen maids were among them.

"COME, SHADOW, COME!" CALLED SUKIE as she glanced through the garden for a large gray cat. Putting on her dark, lightweight shawl, she stepped out into the unusually warm March morning. Behind her, she shut the back door to the house where she worked as an indentured kitchen maid to Mr. Bramwell, a cabinetmaker.

The smell of salt from Boston Harbor filled the air. The small houses leaned against one another as if to stand up better. Noting them, Sukie was reminded of her mother.

SONS OF LIBERTY—*Patriot groups first organized to protest against British taxes in the 1760s. They began as secret societies, with membership known only to other members, but later worked to build popular support for their cause. Sometimes they resorted to mob actions and attacked Tories or British officials. They were the leaders of the Boston Tea Party.*

ENSIGN—*In the British army, an ensign was a young commissioned officer who was often a teenager. He was assigned to carry the flag.*

"Straighten your back," her mother had always said to her. "A free Negro walks with her head up."

Ahead of Sukie, a crowd hurried toward the Old South Meeting House. Mr. Bramwell and his two apprentices, Ben and Christopher, were in that crowd. Maybe out of curiosity, Shadow had followed them.

"Shadow," Sukie called again, anxious to find him before a British soldier seized the cat to catch rats in the army barracks.

The crowd streamed ahead of her. How she wished that she could be on her way to the meetinghouse to see patriot leaders such as John Hancock and Samuel Adams and hear Dr. Joseph Warren give a fiery speech about the Boston Massacre.

Because Sukie was part of a patriot household, her stomach dropped now at the sight of red-coated officers crowding the meetinghouse doors. What were they doing at this gathering? And so many of them. The hands of the meetinghouse clock were almost at ten.

Suddenly, Sukie saw the cat. She started over to him just as a British ensign strode quickly toward the meetinghouse. Shadow darted across the street; the young officer tripped over him and tumbled through the air. With a cry, the boy fell heavily onto the cobblestones and lay still. Sukie's eyes widened. A raw egg splattered beside him.

Shadow crouched his way back over to the young ensign. The cat lowered his head and lapped up the oozing yolk and white.

As Sukie reached to grab Shadow, the officer flung out a long arm and seized her hem. "Help me up, slave!" he rasped. "Help me up, I say!"

Blood rushed to Sukie's face. "I am not a slave," she said in a high voice. "My mama was freed. I am free."

"A British officer commands you!"

Sukie twisted away, tearing the fabric of her dress. Never would she aid a British officer, especially one who called her "slave."

The officer lay still again. Shadow darted around a rain barrel, and Sukie started after him once more.

Nearly an hour passed while she hunted the cat down streets and up alleys. When she neared the meetinghouse again, she heard British voices inside, shouting, "Fie, oh fie!"

A flock of gulls flew up from a roof. Old South's doors burst open, and people rushed out. Sukie watched Ben and Christopher climb out of an upper-story window and clamber down a rainspout. The crowd moved into the street just as a British regiment, with drums beating, marched past them.

She drew in her breath sharply. What was she doing here? She should not be alone on the streets. People had been warned that British patience was wearing thin. And anyway, she should be home helping the cook prepare the midday meal. Mr. Bramwell had invited several friends to come to the house after the commemoration.

She looked around, then quickly covered her head with her shawl and drew it about her. *I will be like Shadow,* she thought. *No one will see me now.*

Sukie glanced quickly back at the British ensign still lying in the street, now nearly surrounded by fellow officers. She ran for home, the cobblestones bruising her feet through her thin soles.

She had just taken the apple pies from the fireplace oven when Ben and Christopher tramped through the back door.

"Well, look who's here," said Christopher, tossing his wool cap on a chair. "Too bad kitchen maids like you miss all the excitement."

Sukie began arranging cheese and dried fish on a platter. "You mean, look who's *there.* Two brave boys who climbed out of the meetinghouse window."

"The British soldiers shouted 'Fire!'" retorted Ben.

"No, they did not," Sukie said. "I was there. They shouted 'Fie, oh fie!'"

"It's true," said Christopher. "There was no fire. Only British soldiers mocking Mr. Adams for stirring up the crowd about the Boston Massacre."

"Mr. Adams used some words that angered the British," added Ben, unwrapping his scarf.

Christopher glowered at Sukie. "What were you doing there?"

"Shadow is lost. I went out to look for him."

"And did you find him?"

Sukie thought for a moment before she answered. "Yes, but as I did, he tripped a British officer. Then he ran away again. The soldier fell in front of me and"—Sukie shook her head—"he dropped a raw egg."

Ben straightened. "I don't believe you. Why would a soldier of old King George be carrying a raw egg?"

Christopher squinted at both of them. "A signal, perhaps?"

The front door slammed so hard that the hall clock missed a tick. Heavy footsteps and loud voices came from the parlor. "A glass of cider to a good end to today's events," boomed Mr. Bramwell.

"Here, here," cried another man.

Sukie, Ben, and Christopher pressed their heads against the parlor door.

Someone laughed. "Was there a scheme afoot today to arrest our patriot leaders? Some think so. If true, the signal to do it was somehow foiled. John Hancock and Samuel Adams are safe."

"Nonetheless," said a low voice, "this speculation may reveal the British thinking. We Sons of Liberty must urge Hancock and Adams to move to safety in an outlying town."

"Agreed!" said Mr. Bramwell. "But for today, all is well."

Sukie smiled, remembering how Shadow's whiskers had glistened with egg white. Christopher and Ben, stupid as fence posts, stared open-mouthed at her.

Sukie pushed away from the door. She smiled as she lit a candle to enter the dark storeroom for a jar of preserves. Freedom had been in the air today, and how sweet it was.

Glancing through a window, her heart lifted when she saw Shadow winding himself around the gate. The cat raised a paw and looked about before making his way through the greening herb garden and home.

Did you know . . . that in New England, former African American slaves who had bought their freedom or been freed by their owners moved openly among the general public? They were not welcome in churches and schools, however, so they built their own. Working in various occupations, they were farmers, craftsmen, storekeepers, blacksmiths, fishermen, and servants. A sailor and former slave, Crispus Attucks, was one of the five colonists killed in the Boston Massacre.

The Boston Massacre

II
HOSTILITIES BEGIN

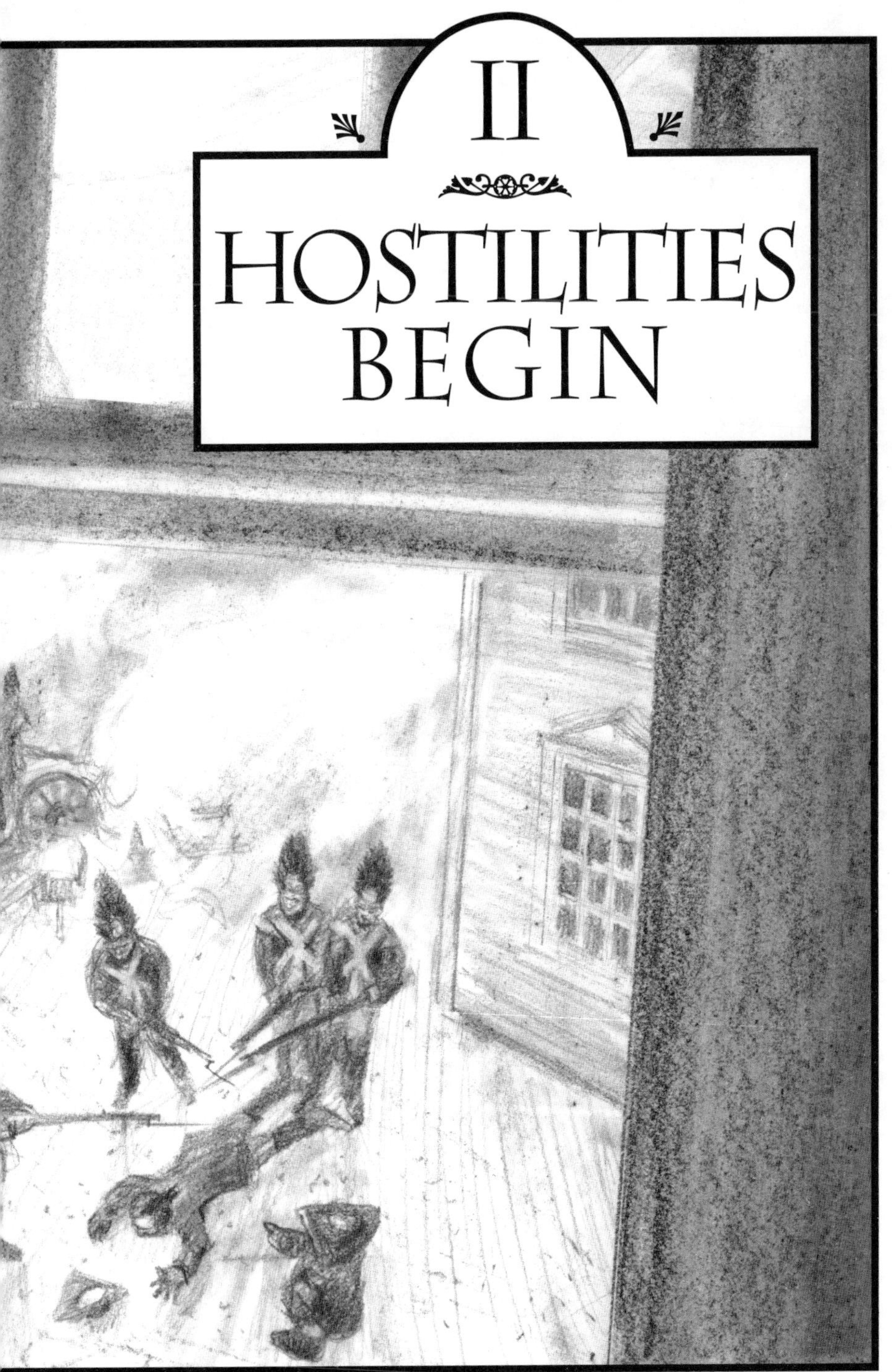

"Just Like a Minuteman" on pages 31–38

NOTHING STOPS PAUL REVERE

by Marcella Fisher Anderson

April 1775 was an unusually warm month. Outside Boston, the colonists planted their vegetable gardens—beets, Lady Finger potatoes, and Tendergreen mustard. Young cattle grazed in the fields. Men of all ages formed citizen militias, ready to defend their homes and farms if the British army should threaten them.

On April 18, 1775, patriot leaders John Hancock and Samuel Adams were in Lexington, Massachusetts, after attending a meeting of the Massachusetts Provincial Congress in Concord, a few miles away. They were staying at the home of one of Hancock's relatives, Reverend Jonas Clarke, before leaving for the Second Continental Congress in Philadelphia.

A few days earlier, rebel spies had learned of British plans to march to Lexington, probably to arrest the two men and seize militia supplies in Concord. Dr. Joseph Warren, head of the Boston Committee of Correspondence, asked Paul Revere—the committee's most trusted rider—to carry a warning to Lexington: the British army was leaving the confines of Boston and was on the march!

RACHEL'S VOICE ROSE UP THE STAIRWAY. "Why can't a younger man carry this message in the dead of night? You have seven children, Paul Revere."

"Yes, and it is for them I ride."

Sarah sat up in bed. Quietly, she crept to the stairs. Under the railing, she watched her father and stepmother in the cold light of the rising April moon.

"I can't understand why you're always the one sent. Ride to New York, ride to Philadelphia, and now tonight, ride to Lexington."

"Maybe I'm the best rider the patriots have." Sarah's father chuckled and ran his finger down his wife's cheek.

Sarah drew back. Rachel Walker had been her stepmother for only a year and a half. Sarah was twelve now, in this year of 1775, and remembered her own mother very well. She remembered her father making that very same gesture to her. Sarah tried to swallow the sudden tightness in her throat. She started quietly back up the stairs.

"Be careful then, Paul," Rachel said gently.

Sarah leaned forward again. Just in time, she saw the door quietly closing and their dog's tail disappearing through the narrowing opening. Sarah could not help herself. "Rachel!" she whispered. "Dog went out, too."

Rachel spun around. "What—Sarah?"

"The dog."

Rachel glanced at Dog's sleeping place by the hearth. "Oh, dear. Yes, well . . . he'll be back by morning. I can't risk opening the door again. It's nearly bright as day out there and time for the British night patrols to be out. You might as well come down," she went on briskly. "We'll have a cup of mint tea. There's a blanket by the fire."

As Sarah lifted the steaming mug, she watched Rachel. Rachel was different from her own mother. More spirited, perhaps. Sarah set down her mug and smiled. Her own mother would never have stood up to her father that way. Still, Sarah's heart ached when she thought of her. Would it never stop aching?

While Rachel was up in the bedroom tending to the crying of baby Joshua, Sarah heard a *scratch-scratch* at the door. What could it be? Dare she open the door when Rachel had already cautioned her against it? *Scratch-scratch.*

Carefully, Sarah slid the bolt. With a chill blast of air, Dog ran in and sat down panting at Sarah's feet. A rolled piece of paper hung from his collar. Sarah untied it just as Rachel came down the stairs.

"Read it, Sarah."

Sarah unrolled the note. She read it aloud. "'*Tie my spurs to Dog's collar and send him back to me.*' . . . Father's spurs!"

"Get them quickly, Sarah."

Sarah tripped twice over the corner of her blanket as she hurried to the back room. Her father's spurs hung from a wall peg and shone in the moonlight.

Rachel ripped the narrow sash from her apron and handed it to Sarah. "Tie them now. Hurry. Can you imagine? Forgetting his spurs!"

Sarah's fingers were all thumbs. At last she made a final knot. She scooted Dog to the door and opened it quietly.

Two men were walking down the street. Sarah knew they

were **Tories.** She dared not make the noise of the latch clicking, so she held the door open barely a crack and waited.

"What fools these colonists are," Sarah could hear through the door, "thinking they can fight the king's finest troops. Tomorrow may be their chance to find out what they're up against."

The voices faded. Sarah wondered where the British patrols were tonight. What did the men mean about tomorrow? She held her breath and opened the door again. The street was empty. Then she slapped Dog on his hindquarters. "Now go," she whispered urgently. "Go back to Father."

Through the crack, Sarah watched Dog as he ran out to the street. Tail waving, he turned in the direction of the Charles River. With her heart still pounding, Sarah went over to the fire. She poked the embers and sat with the blanket around her. She had no thought of sleep now, and she knew that Rachel would stay awake also. Still, as the hours passed, she slept fitfully, waking at last to the sound of Rachel crying softly.

Sarah did not know how to comfort her. She left her place by the fire and walked over to the small window. It was nearly morning. In the early light, she saw the apple trees in bloom, the grass greening in the yards. "I see it now," she said aloud.

TORIES—*Colonists who supported the British during the American Revolution. They were also called Loyalists.*

"What do you see?" asked Rachel, wiping her cheek. "The dawn?"

"I see that you love him, too."

Rachel crossed the floor so quietly that Sarah hardly heard her until she stood behind Sarah. "He is a joy of my life, as you are a joy of his."

Sarah felt hot tears on her own cheeks. Then she turned to Rachel, who held her close.

A scratching sound came at the door. Sarah rushed to open it.

Dog bounded into the room. His collar was empty.

Rachel sat quickly in a chair and laughed. "All is well," she said to Sarah. "Once he is on horseback, nothing will stop Paul Revere."

Did you know . . . that there is no evidence that Paul Revere shouted, "The British are coming"? In April 1775, the colonists still considered themselves British. It is more probable that he and the many other riders that night warned that the regulars or king's men were coming.

Paul Revere's ride on April 18, 1775

JUST LIKE A MINUTEMAN

by Elizabeth Weiss Vollstadt

Once he reached Lexington, Paul Revere—together with fellow rider William Dawes; patriots Samuel Adams, John Hancock, and Jonas Clarke; and members of the Lexington militia—decided that Concord must be alerted as well. The British soldiers, called regulars, wouldn't stop in Lexington. They were after the food, ammunition, and other supplies the militias had stockpiled. Although Revere had warned the citizens of Concord ten days earlier that such an expedition was coming, he and Dawes rode off again to say that this was the night. Other riders, too, such as Samuel Prescott, helped spread the news that the British regulars were coming. Bells tolled. ***Minutemen and militiamen*** *in scattered villages grabbed their muskets.*

In Lexington, the militiamen were waiting at the Buckman Tavern on the village green. When the British arrived, militia leader Captain John Parker saw that his men were greatly outnumbered—approximately 850 British regulars against about 75 Lexington militiamen. He ordered his men to disperse. Then a shot rang out. More shots followed. In the end, eight militiamen lay dead, and nine were wounded. The British continued their march to Concord. There things would be different.

According to Lemuel Shattuck's History of the Town of Concord *(1835), a young girl named Hannah Barns played a small but significant role in the events of the day when she stood up to British soldiers at Ephraim Jones's tavern. The Hannah in this story is based on Shattuck's account. So is the scene where*

British troops point their bayonets at tavern keeper Jones. But the author, not history, places Henry Gardner in the tavern during the early-morning hours of April 19.

THUMP, THUMP! HANNAH'S BROWN EYES FLEW OPEN as she awoke. The sky was still black on this April morning in 1775, but a bright moon shone through her attic window.

Thump, thump! More pounding on her door. "Hannah!" It was Ephraim Jones, keeper of the inn and tavern where Hannah was a servant girl. "Make haste and come downstairs. The redcoats are marching to Concord to seize our guns and supplies. I need you to help serve food and drink to the minutemen."

Hannah leaped out of bed and dressed quickly, shivering in the cold night air. The sound of voices drifted up from the tavern below. She wished she could be a

MINUTEMEN AND MILITIAMEN—*Citizen soldiers who trained to defend their villages and farms from any enemy. Service in the militia was a long tradition in New England, and most towns had a militia made up of all able-bodied men between the ages of sixteen and fifty. In 1774, with trouble brewing with Britain, the Provincial Congress suggested that some militiamen be organized into "minute companies" that could be ready to march on a minute's notice. These minutemen usually trained more often and more vigorously than other militiamen. Many towns had both a standing militia and minutemen.*

minuteman. Serving meals to the soldiers wasn't very exciting. She wanted to be part of the struggle for freedom, too. Sighing, she twisted her long dark hair and pushed it under her cap, then hurried down the wooden stairs.

Soon she was rushing back and forth from the kitchen to the tavern. She took an extra plate of the previous night's meat pie to Henry Gardner, her favorite guest. Mr. Gardner was an important man with serious responsibilities. He was treasurer of the Provincial Congress, a group of men who directed patriot affairs in Massachusetts. But he always had a smile for her.

Once while she was sweeping his room, he came home from a meeting, carrying a large pouch. He used a big key to open the padlock on a heavy chest in the corner. Hannah looked inside. She saw some papers filled with writing. She also saw stacks of gold coins. Mr. Gardner emptied more coins from the pouch into the chest. Then he closed it firmly and clicked the padlock shut.

"The future of the colonies might rest in that chest," he said to Hannah. "Those coins are tax money from the people. I am keeping it safe. If we have to fight the British, we'll need every penny."

He touched Hannah's shoulder. "You can help keep the chest safe. Tell Mr. Jones if you see anyone go into my room."

Every day, Hannah made sure Mr. Gardner's door was tightly closed. She watched for anyone entering his room. She wanted to show him and Mr. Jones that she could do her part, just like a minuteman. But her chance never came.

Now, as she set his plate before him, Mr. Gardner spoke

to her again. "I must leave soon, Hannah," he whispered. "The British officers must not find me here. But my chest is still upstairs."

He leaned close to whisper. "Remember how important it is."

Hannah nodded. She wouldn't forget.

Just then, a messenger flung open the door. "The redcoats fired on our men in Lexington and marched on! They're almost here!"

The minutemen and other militiamen grabbed their weapons and rushed outside. When the tavern was empty, Hannah climbed the stairs to her room. She stood on her bed to look out the high open window. The sun was up over the hills. She could see the road from Lexington. A company of colonial militia was retreating back to town.

Close behind came the British. Line after line of the hated red coats glowed in the early-morning sun. There were so many she couldn't count them. The minutemen and militiamen gathered in the hills around the town. They stood and watched the British soldiers get closer to Concord.

Soon the village square was filled with bright red coats. Hannah's heart began to beat just like the soldiers' drums.

"Search the town," shouted a British officer on horseback. "Look for muskets, cannon, powder, and musket balls. Destroy food and tools that an army could use."

Hannah watched the soldiers break open barrels of flour. They dumped musket balls into the stream. They piled wooden shovels and tools in the village square.

Suddenly, she heard angry voices from the yard below. "This is private property," Mr. Jones was saying. "You cannot enter."

"Out of my way, rebel!" said the British officer. Then there was silence.

Hannah crept down the stairs to the kitchen door. She peered into the jail yard next door. Mr. Jones was lying on the ground. Five soldiers guarded him, their bayonets glinting in the sun. Two others searched the yard. They found three cannon hidden in a pile of firewood. Throwing the logs aside, they dragged the cannon out and smashed their wheels.

Hannah drew back behind the door. She had to think.

The officer came back. "Search the inn," he ordered.

Hannah's mind raced. *Maybe I can't help Mr. Jones,* she thought, *but I can do something. I can hide Mr. Gardner's chest.*

She dashed back up the stairs and slipped into Mr. Gardner's room. She closed the door, then tried to hide the chest behind it. She shoved and shoved until her muscles ached, but the chest was too heavy to move.

Loud footsteps clomped up the wooden stairs. They stopped outside Mr. Gardner's room. Hannah ran to bolt the door, just as it flew open. A British soldier stood in the doorway. "Move aside," he said. "I want to search this room."

Hannah's heart pounded, but she blocked his way. "This is my room," she blurted out. "There's nothing here."

"I'll look for myself," said the soldier.

He grabbed Hannah's arm. She thought of Mr. Jones lying on the ground downstairs. She thought of the minutemen. They needed more men and supplies—and this chest could provide the money for both. She didn't move.

"You can see from here," she said. "The room is empty. There's just a bed and my chest."

"I'll look inside the chest. Hand me the key."

Hannah's stomach turned over. She had no key. But she pretended to look in her apron pocket.

Another soldier came. "What's taking so long?" he demanded. "We're finished here. We let the innkeeper go."

The first soldier pointed into the room. "I want to open that chest," he said.

Hannah's hands were shaking in her apron pocket. "I . . . I can't find the key," she said.

The soldier held up his musket. "Then I'll break the lock."

"Wait!" said the other soldier. "The officers are already angry because some soldiers have stolen private property."

The first soldier put down his musket. His eyes stayed on the chest.

The second soldier spoke again. "What could be in a young girl's chest?"

Hannah could see that he wanted to leave. "Just my churchgoing dress and my grandmother's shawl," she said. "I'd show you if I had my key. I could see if I dropped it in the kitchen."

The soldier laughed harshly. "I don't think our officers

want your grandmother's shawl." He turned and walked toward the stairs.

The first soldier looked from Hannah to the chest and back to Hannah. Her knees trembled. Her hands shook behind her apron. But her eyes stayed still and calm. Finally, the soldier turned and stomped down the stairs. Hannah bolted the door and sank to the floor. Her trembling legs could hold her no longer, but she had done it. She had saved Mr. Gardner's chest.

She closed her eyes and leaned heavily against the door. Minutes later, she leaped to her feet, gripped by a new fear. The smell of smoke drifted through the room's open window. She raced upstairs to her attic room, where she could see the village square. A bonfire blazed, sending smoldering ashes into the sky. Soon the fire spread to the roof of the nearby courthouse.

Through the smoke, Hannah could see the minutemen and militiamen leave the hills. They must have seen the smoke, too. They marched toward the British soldiers at the North Bridge. They were coming to save the town. Then she heard the sound of muskets firing. Still, the colonials kept coming across the bridge. Hannah knew there was no turning back now. The fight had begun.

Much later, when the sun had set, minutemen drifted back into the tavern. They were tired and dirty, but their spirits were high. They smiled as Hannah poured cold cider from an earthen pitcher. "We showed those redcoats," said one, holding up his glass. "We chased them back to Boston."

"A job well done," said Mr. Jones, as he placed a pot of

stew on the table. "I am proud to serve you all." Then he took the pitcher from Hannah and pointed to an empty place on the wooden bench.

"Come sit," he said to her, pouring another glass of cider. "I am proud to serve you, too." He turned to the minutemen. "Hannah is also a brave soldier. She told me how she kept the redcoats from opening Henry Gardner's chest. Now the money to supply our army is safe."

Hannah sat down and slowly drank the sweet cider. A wide smile spread across her face. Tomorrow she would be a servant girl again. But today she was a brave soldier—just like a minuteman.

Did you know . . . that Henry Wadsworth Longfellow's famous poem "Paul Revere's Ride" is not historically accurate? Paul Revere did not ride alone. William Dawes slipped out of Boston by another route and also aroused the countryside. The two men met at Lexington and continued on to Concord. Along the way, they met Samuel Prescott, who had been visiting with his fiancée in Lexington and was heading home to Concord. The three men were spotted by British officers. Dawes galloped away but was thrown from his horse when the animal took fright at something and stopped suddenly. Dawes then got up and slipped away. Revere was surrounded and captured. Only Prescott, riding a strong fresh horse, escaped to finish the ride to Concord. Shortly thereafter, alarmed that the countryside was awake and waiting for the regulars, the British officers took Revere's horse and released him.

THE DAY THE BELL RANG

by Richard E. Albert

Events moved quickly after the April 1775 fighting at Lexington and Concord. John Hancock and Samuel Adams reached Philadelphia safely by May 10 to attend the Second Continental Congress. On the same date, Benedict Arnold and Ethan Allen captured British-held Fort Ticonderoga on Lake Champlain in New York. A month later, on June 17, Boston patriots fought the British in the Battle of Breed's and Bunker Hills, holding their own until their ammunition ran out.

Three major results came out of the Second Continental Congress. First, on June 15, George Washington was appointed commander in chief of the Continental army. Second, the delegates tried to persuade the British to consider the colonists' grievances as recorded in the Olive Branch Petition. Their words were never read. Finally, the delegates became increasingly aware of the rising anger of the colonists and their own growing frustrations with Britain.

Throughout the colonies, events moved closer toward support for independence. On January 24, 1776, American General Henry Knox arrived in Boston with forty-three artillery pieces and sixteen cannons pulled by oxen from Fort Ticonderoga. The emplacement of this artillery on a height above the city and harbor led to the British evacuation of Boston on March 17, 1776. Fighting broke out in other regions, too. The British launched a naval attack on Charleston, South Carolina, on June 28, 1776, but were repulsed by the colonials.

By June 1776, when Congress met again in Philadelphia,

demands for independence could no longer be ignored. On June 7, Richard Henry Lee of Virginia proposed a resolution that the colonies "are, and of right ought to be, free and independent states." Recognizing a need for further discussion, Congress decided to postpone a vote on the resolution. At the same time, they appointed a committee to prepare a document that would not only declare independence from Britain but also list their grievances against the mother country and describe their views of a just government.

The committee was composed of Thomas Jefferson of Virginia, John Adams of Massachusetts, Robert Livingston of New York, Benjamin Franklin of Pennsylvania, and Roger Sherman of Connecticut. They agreed that Jefferson should write the first draft of the document, then submit it to them for revision. On July 2 and 3, Congress made further changes in the document. At last, on July 4, Congress voted unanimously for the amended version of the Declaration of Independence.

As president of Congress, John Hancock was the only delegate who signed the document on that day. By August, after the Declaration had been copied onto fine parchment, almost all the delegates had signed it.

The Declaration of Independence was read aloud from the State House steps to the people of Philadelphia on July 8. After the reading, the State House bell rang out so loudly that farmers in their fields could hear it ringing and hurried to town to be part of the great celebration.

ENOCH HAD JUST GONE TO THE BROOK to get a bucket of water when he heard the bell. He stood for a moment listening. Even though it was far away, the sound was clear and mellow, echoing across the countryside. It was July 8, 1776.

Setting his bucket on the ground, Enoch turned abruptly and stepped along a log that spanned the narrow stream. Then he ran toward the field where his father was working.

"Father," he shouted, "the bell in the State House is ringing!"

His father had heard it, too. Turning away from his plow, he looked in the direction of Philadelphia, which lay in the distance along the banks of the Delaware River.

"Do you think it's the celebration the peddler was talking about?" Enoch asked his father.

"Could be."

Enoch remembered the man with the scraggly horse and loaded wagon, who had stopped by the farm four days ago, bringing news from Philadelphia. He had said that important people were still meeting in the Continental Congress at the State House.

Enoch wondered if one of them was Thomas Paine. Enoch's father had nailed a copy of Paine's pamphlet, *Common Sense,* just inside the barn door so he could read a little bit of it every day.

"Will the decisions of these important people bring changes to the land?" Enoch had asked.

"Yes, indeed," the peddler replied, urging his horse forward. "A cause for celebration, lad."

"Could this be the celebration day? Can we go to see what's happening?" he asked his father now. He thought of all the people who would be gathering in the square on this July morning and of the excitement of being there.

"Don't have time," his father answered crisply. "Late plowing this hay field as it is."

Though disappointed, Enoch knew how important it was to get the crops planted on time.

"Could I go myself?" Enoch asked suddenly. He realized it was some distance, but it would be worth the four-mile walk to find out what the celebration was about.

"Well, now, Enoch, I don't know," his father answered slowly, pondering the request. "But if you're willing to try, I can't see any reason why you shouldn't. Be sure to start back in time so you'll get home before dark."

Enoch jammed his straw hat down on his head and set out on the road. The sun shimmered off the barn roofs. He was excited but still wondering about what the man had told his father and about the important people meeting in the State House. They had come not only from Massachusetts but also from other distant places, such as Virginia and New York. It would have taken them many days to reach Philadelphia.

As he drew near the city, he saw pillars of smoke rising in the air. In a moment of fright, he wondered if the city was burning and the bell had been ringing to warn the people of the fire.

He started running to see for himself. Then, entering the street leading to the square, he saw that the smoke was from many bonfires. They, too, must be part of the celebration.

As he moved through the crowd gathered around the State House, the thrill of being there energized him. Men, women, and children—tiny ones carried in their parents' arms, older ones gazing in wonder as he did—were milling about. Some boys his own age shouted and threw sticks into the bonfires.

Enoch thought of joining them, hoping they would let him take part in their fun. But he was so awestruck that he only watched. It was hard to believe there could be so many people in Philadelphia—even in the entire colony.

He climbed a tree to have a better view. From near the top, he could see the man still ringing the great bell in the State House belfry.

Then he noticed three men approaching the tree. They stopped for a minute to talk. One, an elderly gentleman, turned and saw Enoch up in the tree. The man left his friends and walked over.

"I always like a boy who climbs a tree to see things better," he said to Enoch. "Do you know what this is all about?"

Enoch shook his head, astounded to find that this man knew exactly what he was wondering. The gentleman had a kind face, with little wrinkles around his eyes when he smiled and graying hair that dropped to the back of his collar. He lowered his spectacles to look up at Enoch in the tree.

"This is indeed a great time, lad," he said.

"But what are all these people doing?" Enoch asked. "And why does the great bell in the State House ring? And why are all the bonfires burning?"

"Perhaps you don't know it," the elderly gentleman said, "but we have declared ourselves independent from Britain. You'll be living in a new country from now on."

Enoch dropped down from a low branch. A new country? How could it be? The road he had traveled into Philadelphia, the streets, the State House were all the same as they had been the last time he had come to the city. His own home on the farm, the fields his father plowed, the brook that ran by the house—they were no different from what they had always been. There were the same green maples in this early part of summer, the same bright buttercups, and the same sunny days.

What did the man mean by a new country? How could it be, when it was exactly the same as it had been for as long as he could remember?

"I don't understand, sir," he said, puzzled. "Won't I be living in Pennsylvania anymore?"

"You will still be living in Pennsylvania," the man replied, "though it will no longer be a colony but a state, part of a new nation. Four days ago, a document was adopted by the Continental Congress. It is called the Declaration of Independence. At twelve noon today, it was read aloud from the State House steps."

Enoch looked again at the blazing bonfires. Now he could hear *all* the church bells ringing. "What will this new nation be called?" Enoch asked the elderly gentleman.

The other two men had finished talking, and they turned to look for their companion. "Are you coming, Mr. Franklin?" one of them asked.

"I'll be with you shortly," said the elderly man as he turned to Enoch, a twinkle lighting up his eyes behind his spectacles.

Enoch's own eyes opened wide. He was talking with the great Benjamin Franklin! He must listen carefully.

"The new nation, lad," Mr. Franklin said finally, "will be called the United States of America."

Later that afternoon, Enoch didn't follow the road back home. He traveled cross-country, moving swiftly between rows of corn and splashing through streams, until at last he saw his father stopped by the plow and drinking water from a jug.

"Independence, Father!" hollered Enoch. "A new nation!"

A flock of startled mallards rose and flew straight across the reddening sky.

"I heard all about it in town. Mr. Franklin himself told me." Enoch threw his hat into the air. "Independence!"

Did you know . . . that Thomas Paine was a poor Englishman who worked at various trades to earn a meager living? In 1774, he met Benjamin Franklin, who was on official business in London. Franklin encouraged Paine to go to America. Once there, Paine wrote several pamphlets in support of the American cause. One, titled *Common Sense,* was published in January 1776. Paine's writings helped shape the political thinking of America's patriot leaders. Equally important, the clarity and passion of his writings convinced ordinary citizens of the need to fight for independence. More than 150,000 copies of *Common Sense* were sold. The pamphlet was published in twenty-five editions by a number of printers, passed from hand to hand, and carried by peddlers into every colony.

III

THE REVOLUTION IN THE NORTH

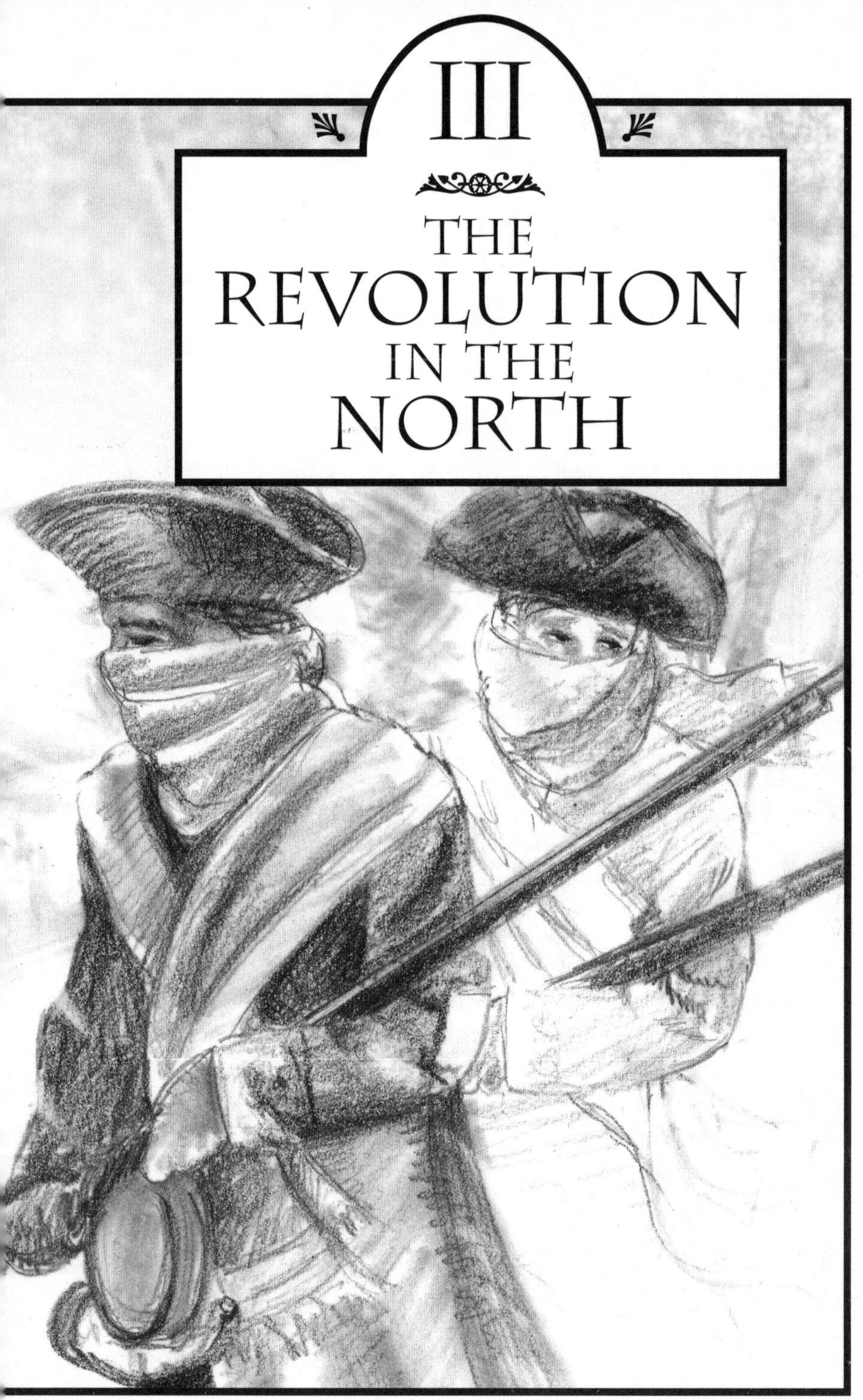

"A Soldier Is Born" on pages 65–75

ACROSS THE DELAWARE

by Marcella Fisher Anderson

After the patriots celebrated the passage of the Declaration of Independence in July 1776, the Continental army met with serious military defeats. General Washington's twenty thousand poorly trained and ill-equipped men faced more than forty-five thousand professional British troops commanded by General William Howe in the New York City area.

Howe defeated the Americans at Brooklyn Heights, sending Washington's troops into a panic and inflicting heavy casualties. Had bad weather not interfered with the orders given to Admiral Richard Howe (General Howe's brother) to sail up the East River and cut off an American retreat, Washington's entire army might have been captured. Instead, Washington escaped across the East River with ninety-five hundred men during the night of August 29.

General Howe delayed pursuing Washington's army. With authority from George III, he proposed an informal peace conference. Congress assigned Benjamin Franklin, John Adams, and Edmund Rutledge to meet with Admiral Howe. The conference took place on Staten Island on September 11. Any hope of negotiation ended abruptly when Howe insisted at the outset that the Declaration of Independence be revoked.

Still in New York State, Washington continued to withdraw, building fortifications on Harlem Heights. There he almost lost a large part of his army when he was outflanked by the British. He was then forced to withdraw to White Plains. On October 28, the Continentals were defeated again.

During this period, Washington's primary objective was to hold his small army together. His troops continued their retreat through New Jersey. On December 7 and 8, they crossed the Delaware River into Pennsylvania, where the British ended their chase.

Howe and his army returned to New York City for the winter. He believed that he had destroyed the patriots' spirit and will to fight. Planning to put a quick end to the revolt in the spring, he ordered his Hessian troops into winter quarters in New Jersey. One town, Trenton, was defended by some fourteen hundred Hessian soldiers under Colonel Johann Rahl.

Washington made plans to cross the Delaware River with twenty-four hundred men on Christmas Day, 1776, and launch an attack on Trenton. The night before the army moved, he ordered that a copy of Thomas Paine's pamphlet The American Crisis, No. 1, *be read aloud at every campfire. Paine had written his stirring words while retreating with Washington's army across New Jersey. The pamphlet begins, "These are the times that try men's souls."*

Desperate for success, Washington sent his men into battle with the password "Victory or Death." Meanwhile, Colonel Rahl and his men began sleeping off their Christmas celebration. But in the Pennsylvania and New Jersey countryside, not everyone was asleep.

ON CHRISTMAS NIGHT, 1776, James held his dog, Scout, close to him and raised his head above the side of the boat where he was hiding. Cargo rafts, ferries, and iron ore carriers crowded close to the Pennsylvania side of the Delaware River. James looked across to the New Jersey shore. Through the snow, he tried to see a candle burning in his mother's pantry window.

Suddenly, a strong hand grabbed his damp collar. "What are you doing here?" a sentry whispered harshly.

"And a dog besides. Keep him quiet and follow me."

"I've only one mind, sir—to cross the river for home," said James, hurrying to follow the sentry to his commanding officer.

"I found him, I did, in one of the boats, sir. Give him your name, lad."

"James Morris." Remembering that his father had fought bravely against the British and died at White Plains, James added, "Patriot."

The officer's gaze softened. "Well, James Morris, you have discovered us in the midst of a surprise crossing of the Delaware tonight. You will have to come with us."

"Scout and I have crossed this river many times."

"Muzzle that dog, O'Hara," the officer said to the sentry, "and put them both next to the helmsman on the first boat. Young Morris may be useful."

In the stern of the boat, James rubbed Scout's nose where the rag strip was tied to keep him from barking. James thought of home and the October day he and his mother had learned of his father's death. Soon afterward, his mother had sent James across the river to her parents' farm, thinking the change would be good for him. But James knew now that that had been the wrong thing for him to do. He had never fully faced the fact of his father's death. He knew he should go home, but he was still afraid—afraid to face the empty chair and the dark hearth where his father had always built a high fire, a better one than James felt he could ever make.

"A fine way to spend Christmas night," said the helmsman quietly, interrupting James's thoughts. "A hard crossing even with us fishermen from Marblehead manning the boats."

"Where did all the boats come from?" asked James softly.

"From Captain Daniel Bray and other men," whispered the helmsman. "On Washington's orders, they stole the boats at night, floated them downriver here, then hid them. Twenty-four hundred men are crossing tonight. We'll thrash those **Hessians** at Trenton."

James heard the clatter of horses coming aboard, then felt a lunge beneath him as the boat was poled and rowed out onto the river. "The current will be swiftest closer to the other shore," he warned the helmsman.

Scout stirred in James's arms. Presently, a faint glow shone from Johnson's ferry house dead ahead. Close to land now, the Marbleheaders fought against the current.

As the boats neared the opposite bank, men in the dark reached for the mooring lines. James stared. "Tories!" he said aloud. He recognized them as his mother's neighbors,

HESSIANS*—German soldiers who were hired by the British to fight for them. Most of the Hessian victories came during the early fighting in New York State, but throughout the conflict they were generally feared by the Americans. The Hessian presence made Loyalists feel uneasy because they had expected to be entirely protected by British troops. During the war, the Continental Congress printed propaganda pamphlets written in German that encouraged the Hessians to desert the British. When the war ended, nearly five thousand Hessians settled in the new nation.*

who supported Britain's king. James's heart stopped.

"It's no treachery, young Morris," said one of the men, grasping a horse's bridle. "We no longer trust the British. We're patriots now. Except for Krock. Strange one, he is."

He gestured to a heavyset man slinking into the shadows. Alarmed, James watched the Tory, Krock, disappear into the woods. Sentries chased after him, but James knew that Krock could evade them.

Leaving Scout unmuzzled and snuffling about the guarded ferry house, James started tracking the Tory.

Snow alternated with sleet. A strong wind carried the sound of a church bell. One in the morning. The crossing was taking longer than planned, moving the surprise attack into daylight hours. James's head throbbed.

Two miles, from tree to tree, he followed the spy Krock until at last the Tory headed for the ice-covered rock ledges that James himself climbed in summer to take a shortcut to Trenton.

James circled swiftly around the rocks, reaching the ledges just as Krock stretched for one last handhold. He stepped on the man's hands. "Up or down, Tory?" James's heart pounded. What would he do now?

The man's lips parted over his teeth. "Rebel vermin," Krock muttered as he tried to free his hands.

There was a movement in the woods below, and suddenly a brown bundle of energy growled its way up the rocks and leaped, fastening itself onto the man's ankle.

Krock's eyes widened in surprise. "Off, beast!" he cried, losing his handhold and grazing the rocks as he fell backward onto the snow below.

James tore down and around the ledges, reaching the man as he staggered to his feet and rocked unsteadily. "March, Tory," James said, prodding the dazed man with a sharp, heavy stick he had picked up off the ground.

"The rebels will not succeed tonight." Krock laughed, swaying a little. "Their muskets are too wet to fire." He twisted his head and spat at James's feet.

James prodded him harder in the ribs. "Back to the river, traitor."

From Johnson's ferry house, the lanterns shone with an icy brilliance. Krock lunged to escape. James stretched out his stick and tripped him.

The Tory struggled to regain his footing but slipped on the ice-crusted snow. With a bellow, he rolled helplessly down the hill to the river. Scout and James ran beside him.

A familiar sentry rushed from behind the ferry house. "Guard him, O'Hara," James shouted with triumph that rang in the frozen air. "He's a spy. I know him well!"

Soon, in the early light, James slogged wearily home. He paused at his father's garden, where dry cornstalks rattled in the wind. He thought about the times he and his father had laughed and hidden from each other in the rows of tall corn. Remembering brought hot tears to James's eyes.

But James took a deep breath and, with Scout following, crossed the yard toward the candle in the window. It was time to be here to help his mother, time to face the empty chair and the hearth. James knew he could do that now.

It was time to be home.

Do you wonder . . . whether the British ever received warnings about American attacks? Colonel Johann Rahl received one on Christmas night. A Tory delivered a note to his headquarters informing him that the Americans were crossing the Delaware. Involved in a game of cards, Rahl set the note aside, unread. Rahl was wounded in the attack. The note was found in his pocket two days later, when he died of his wounds.

Crossing the Delaware

DARK FOREST DANGER

by Marcella Fisher Anderson

The Battle of Trenton in December 1776 was the first major victory for the Continental army. It was soon followed by a victory at the Battle of Princeton, after which Washington wintered his troops at Morristown, New Jersey. The American and British armies now waited for spring.

On leave in England, General John Burgoyne spent January plotting a military campaign that he believed would end the war by the close of 1777. The strategy called first for British control of Lake Champlain, Fort Ticonderoga, and the Hudson River. After accomplishing these goals, Burgoyne planned to meet two other British generals, William Howe and Barry St. Leger, at Albany, New York. If the plan succeeded, the British would control the Hudson River valley, and New England would be isolated from the rest of the colonies.

The plan was approved in London by Lord George Germain, colonial secretary, and agreed to by Howe and St. Leger. On paper, it was a grand campaign. But when Burgoyne headed south from Canada in the spring of 1777, he faced unknown obstacles. Howe, commander in chief of all British forces in America, decided to sail to Philadelphia to seize the city and the Continental Congress, which was meeting there.

Burgoyne did not learn of the change in Howe's plans until mid-August. Meanwhile, he moved his heavily burdened army through the hot wilderness during the summer of 1777. They maneuvered slowly with a hundred pieces of artillery and a train of supply wagons that included nearly thirty filled with baggage for Burgoyne and his staff. The dense forests provided perfect cover for the rebels' Indian-style raids. The Americans cut down trees to block roads and built dams to flood streams, further slowing the enemy's progress.

Farther west in New York State, St. Leger marched southeast from Oswego and met with unexpected resistance at Oriskany and Fort Stanwix. During both battles in the Mohawk River valley, the patriot militia fought courageously to protect their families, homes, and farms. Eventually deserted by his Mohawk Indian allies, St. Leger retreated to Oswego.

By early August, British supplies were alarmingly low. Learning that military stockpiles were stored to the east in Bennington, a small town in the Hampshire Grants, Burgoyne ordered seven hundred Hessians under Lieutenant Colonel Friedrick Baum to seize the supplies. The Hessians were soundly defeated by the overwhelming patriot force under General John Stark. Burgoyne's army plodded on.

Finally, on September 19, General Horatio Gates's American army clashed with the British at Freeman's Farm, near Saratoga, New York, on the Hudson River. In the ensuing battle, Burgoyne lost six hundred men—troops that he knew he could never replace.

On October 7, Burgoyne launched an attack against the Americans, again at Freeman's Farm. Once more, the British met with determined militia opposition, Daniel Morgan's trusted sharpshooters, and the valiant leadership of American general Benedict Arnold. (These two battles are known variously as the First and Second Battles of Freeman's Farm and the First and Second Battles of Saratoga.)

Hungry, outnumbered, low on supplies, and facing a winter in the wilderness, Burgoyne's troops attempted a brief retreat that failed. On October 17, General Gates accepted the British surrender at Saratoga. Pledged to end their fighting days, Burgoyne's troops were marched to the Atlantic coast. There they were paraded past jeering Bostonians on the way to ships awaiting them. According to the surrender agreement, the prisoners were to be transported back to England.

The wilderness that was such a formidable adversary for the British also posed problems for Americans living on the frontier. Many children, such as those in this story, found it easier than the adults to adapt to the harsh environment.

AS THE WAGON CARRYING THEM LURCHED ALONG the forest road, Bridey leaned over to whisper in her little brother's ear. "Mikey, I'm goin' back to our cabin, I am. To get the brass candlesticks. I forgot them, and Mam needs them. She needs the light."

Mikey's eyes widened. "Bridey, no—no go. Soldiers. Indians."

"I've thought about them. Then I've thought about Mam, too, and I'm goin'." She took his small hand in hers. "I'll think about you and talk to you the whole time I'm gone."

They glanced at their mother. She sat hunched on the driver's box, urging on Aggie, the milk cow, pressed into pulling the wagon. Mam talked in that nonsensical singsong way that she used more and more these days: "Up the road now, Aggie. Catch a toad. Up the road."

Bridey reached over and tousled Mikey's red hair just before she slipped off the splintered tailgate. Mud sucked around her bare feet as she watched the wagon vanish in the morning fog.

Quickly, she dodged between the trees. She thought that surely the way back was not far. Now and then, she stopped to listen to the sounds of movement: British soldiers dragging heavy cannon through the underbrush; the crashing tread of Hessian boots. Deeper in the woods, she heard a wild turkey call that she knew was not real. Daniel Morgan was gathering his rebel sharpshooters. Deeper still within the trees, she also knew that British general Burgoyne's Mohawk Indian allies were moving as silently as yellow maple leaves blowing through the forest.

Suddenly, Bridey stepped out onto the edge of a large clearing. It had once been a farm belonging to Mr. Freeman, a Tory who had abandoned everything and escaped to Canada. A field of ripened wheat stretched from the deserted farm buildings to the woods.

She squinted to see better in the slowly lifting fog. To her left, four British officers stood on the roof of the small barn. The pale sun glinted off the gold braid on their shoulders and the brass spyglasses they held to their eyes. On the ground stood rows of tall British grenadiers with big black hats and white straps crossed over the front of their dull red uniforms. At the rear, artillerymen pulled their guns up closer.

Bridey slapped at the deer flies biting her bare arms, then slipped back into the woods. Oak, beech, and birch trees grew so close together that she could barely see between them. The sun rose higher.

When she looked back again, the four officers were gone. In perfect march formation, the scarlet British lines began to move, trampling the wheat before them.

A wild turkey call drifted again from the woods. "The

British are too dumb to know, Mikey," whispered Bridey as her heart jumped. "Daniel Morgan's men are in those woods. The trees are filled with sharpshooters. Too dumb to know, they are."

Halfway across the field, the British started falling before flashes of rifle fire from the woods. Their lines fell back, regrouped, and moved forward again.

Bridey covered her ears. The battle surged back and forth. She wanted to leave, but something held her there.

Then an American officer on a small brown horse galloped in front of the rebels. He rode hard, waving his sword in the air, rallying them to attack once again.

Soon there was too much smoke to see the battle. Silence fell in some parts of the field. Elsewhere, men cried out. Bridey could watch no longer. She wiped her tears with trembling hands and turned away.

Circling back through the forest away from the battleground, she started once again toward her family's cabin. Even so, danger seemed to filter through the trees.

"Mam must have her candlesticks," she repeated to herself. Only light from the glowing tapers could defeat the forest darkness, the flapping wings of unseen night birds, the howl of wolves around a kill. Bridey had known only the forest, been born in it, but Mam had known and loved the open green pastures and wide sparkling seas off the coast of Ireland. The forest still frightened her.

Bridey's father had left for Fort Ticonderoga to fight the "bloody British" and been taken prisoner. Soon after, Mam made plans to move to Bennington, to be near her sister,

Aunt Nora. Perhaps there, Mam would smile again, thought Bridey as she neared the cabin, and even sing Irish songs to her and Mikey again.

"If I find those candlesticks, Mikey, I promise I will polish them with tallow and river sand every day, I will," she said half aloud.

It was midafternoon before she reached the cabin. There it stood across the rough-cleared field. Corn and bean plants grew stunted in the forest shade.

She lifted the latch. The door squeaked as it fell back on its leather hinges. She closed the door behind her as a shadow crossed the window. She ran over to it and pressed her back against the wall, then carefully lifted the edge of the oiled paper that covered the window. More shadows moved among the trees. "Indians," she whispered. "Oh, Mikey! I think they're Mohawks."

Crouching low, she ran over to a broken pine chest. A glint from behind it caught her eye, and she pulled up the two candlesticks from where they had fallen during her family's rushed departure.

She crept again to the window. Two Mohawks, their faces streaked with red and orange paint, moved silently toward the barn. Her thoughts whirled.

Tearing off her apron, she wrapped the candlesticks inside it. From behind the door, she hauled out a tattered quilt and wrapped it around the bundle in her arms. She had decided what to do: she would pretend she was carrying an infant who had died. Shaking as she cradled the bundle in her arms, she opened the door, willing herself not to look toward the trees. Beside the woodpile, she found two sticks of kindling and a spade. She grasped the sticks and the heavy tool with one hand, dragging the blade behind her, bumping it over the rough ground.

At the corner of the vegetable garden, she laid down the bundle and began to dig, knowing that a hundred eyes watched her from the trees. Maybe among these Indians was the small band that had come to the cabin one winter day two years ago. The snow had been up to the window. Bridey recalled now that Mam had given them fresh milk. They had drunk hungrily from the bucket until little remained. Then Mam had nodded tearfully toward baby Mikey. The Indians had left quietly. "Remember that now," she whispered to the shadows before her in the trees.

When she had dug a hole large enough for the bundle, she tore off her bonnet straps. Using them to tie the two sticks together, she fashioned a cross. Then, after kissing her bundle and holding it close to her racing heart, she laid it in the dug grave.

Bridey found it easy to weep as she covered the bundle with dirt and set the cross atop it. She had failed in trying to get the candlesticks. Burying them like a dead infant was at least better than leaving them for the Indians to steal. Perhaps they would not even disturb the gravesite. Perhaps someday, when the fighting ended, she could return to dig up the candlesticks. Perhaps then Mam would be pleased, would show her that she loved her and always would.

Never glancing back, Bridey straightened her shoulders and walked away, back toward the wagon road they had followed that morning. She had not gone far when an orange light flickered off the white birches in front of her, reflecting the firing of her family's cabin. A flock of passenger pigeons flew across the smoke-dimmed sun.

Bridey ran. She ran until she thought her heart would burst. Scarcely remembering how she found her way, she broke out onto the road. Their wagon stood in a patch of sunlight; it had gone only a short way from where she had left it. Aggie, the cow, turned her head to gaze at her. Bridey stood stunned, her clothes torn, her dark hair hanging loose. Slowly, she took a deep breath and walked toward the wagon.

"Bridey," came a small, tired voice from the road's edge. "Bridey no lost!"

Mam came around the wagon and stared, then started running toward her.

Bridey stood still, her arms held straight down and her hands clenched into fists. "I don't have the candlesticks," she called out before her mother could reach her. "But I buried them from the Indians."

"Oh, but we have you," cried her mother, gathering Bridey into her arms. She held her so close that Bridey could feel the warm tears falling on her head. "We have you, Bridey, my love. We have you."

Feeling Mikey's thin, hard arms tightening around her legs, Bridey pressed her face against Mam and cried, too.

Did you know . . . that the American officer Bridey saw was Benedict Arnold, one of George Washington's most brilliant generals? He was feared by the British for his military strategy and ferocity in battle. In May 1775, he was a commander in the capture of Fort Ticonderoga and the British garrison stationed there. Later that year, September to December 1775, he led an ill-fated expedition into Canada. In the spring of 1776, the Americans retreated to Lake Champlain. There, Arnold built a fleet of sorts and commanded two naval battles against the British. While the Americans did not win a victory, they did succeed in stopping the British from advancing south. In late fall, the British commander feared winter's approach and led his troops back to Canada.

The most stunning of Arnold's exploits was the American victory at Saratoga in October 1777, a victory due largely to Arnold's heroic attacks against Burgoyne's army. Arnold felt that he was not receiving due recognition for his daring actions, however, and became embittered. In 1779, he began passing secret information to the British. Then, in 1780, he turned traitor to the American cause when he schemed to betray West Point, a strategic military base, which he commanded. The plot was foiled when a fellow conspirator, British major John André, was captured while carrying the plans for the betrayal. Arnold escaped to the British army, which gave him a monetary reward and a commission as a general. Even so, he lived out his life in England, an impoverished and broken man.

Do you wonder . . . if all Indians supported the British? The answer is no; some supported the patriots, which caused old alliances to falter. The Mohawks who helped the British at Saratoga were members of the Iroquois Confederacy, an alliance of six Indian nations—Mohawks, Oneidas, Tuscaroras, Onondagas, Cayugas, and Senecas. This alliance had been formed for common defense and combined influence against the encroaching white settlers. With the coming of the American Revolution, the Confederacy broke apart over disagreements as to whether to support the British or American sides. The Mohawks and Senecas fought on the side of the British against the Americans. The other tribes, especially the Oneidas and Cayugas, gave active, loyal support to the patriots.

Do you wonder . . . What made the Battle of Saratoga so important? After the victory, France decided to come into the Revolution on the side of the United States. In early 1778, the French agreed to an alliance with America, sending arms, men, and money in support. The French navy was a formidable ally against the British fleet.

A SOLDIER IS BORN

by Elizabeth Weiss Vollstadt

The victory at Saratoga proved that colonial soldiers could defeat the better-trained, better-equipped British troops. But the war was not over yet. Farther south, in Pennsylvania, things weren't going well for General George Washington. On September 11, 1777, his forces were defeated at Chadds Ford, on Brandywine Creek. Two weeks later, on September 26, the British advanced into Philadelphia, forcing the Continental Congress to flee west to the town of York. In October, the Continental army was defeated yet again, this time at Germantown.

As Christmas drew near, British general William Howe and his men were settled in Philadelphia, warm and well fed. By contrast, Washington and his army of thirteen thousand men were marching in biting winds and snow to Valley Forge, where they would spend the winter. The men were poorly dressed; more than one thousand of them had no shoes. They arrived at Valley Forge a few days before Christmas with only tents for shelter and little food. One young soldier, Joseph Plumb Martin wrote, "We arrived at the Valley Forge in the evening. It was dark. There was no water to be found and I was perishing with thirst. I searched for water till I was weary and came to my tent without finding any. Fatigue and thirst, joined with hunger, almost made me desperate." These harsh conditions were only a taste of what was to come.

Washington had already given orders that the men be divided into squads of twelve and that each group should build a log hut for itself. The huts were small by today's standards—14 feet wide, 16 feet long, and 6½ feet high. Two walls had bunks, one a fireplace, and the fourth a door. The men began building the huts a few days before Christmas, and within three weeks many were completed.

The huts were better than tents, but they were still cramped and drafty. Adding to the suffering was a shortage of food. The men were supposed to have daily rations of a pint of milk, a quart of beer, peas, beans, butter, a pound of bread, and a pound of either meat or fish. But they frequently did not receive rations even close to that. A flour-water mixture cooked on a griddle, called ***firecake****, was sometimes the only food they had.*

Many men became sick, and some died. Hundreds deserted, although most deserters were recent immigrants or former British soldiers. Most American-born soldiers felt a deep loyalty to the cause. Young Joseph Martin wrote, "We had engaged in the defense of our injured country and we were determined to persevere as long as such hardships were not altogether intolerable."

The men did endure, and somehow, despite the difficulties of that winter, the Continental army emerged stronger and more unified. One reason for this was the leadership and example set by Washington. Another was the presence of Baron Friedrich von Steuben, a former soldier in the Prussian army of Frederick the Great. Von Steuben taught the Continentals improved methods of marching, loading and firing their weapons, and using their bayonets. Many people say that the Continental army was born at Valley Forge.

FIRECAKE*—A simple, unleavened bread that many men in the Continental army at Valley Forge ate to keep from starving. It consisted of flour mixed with water and salt (if they had it) and was cooked on a griddle or stone.*

"I'M QUITTIN' THIS ARMY—if you can call it that—soon as my enlistment's up next month," Patrick said to his cousin Thomas as they trudged toward the woods behind their camp. "I can chop trees at home as well as here."

He shivered as melting snow seeped into his worn boots, soaking his already icy feet and toes. Would this long winter at Valley Forge never end? The March sun might hint of spring, but Patrick felt as if he'd never be warm again.

"You can't quit!" Thomas protested. "General Washington needs every man and boy who can shoot a musket! You must stay and help us lick the redcoats."

"The only ones gettin' licked are us," Patrick growled. He pointed to a company of men in tattered clothes drilling nearby. Most ignored the beat of the drum as they plodded around the muddy, snow-dotted field. "Look at them now. Do they look like an army? And our Pennsylvania brigade is no better."

The previous summer, when they had both turned sixteen, Patrick had been as eager as Thomas to join the Continental army. But the defeats at Brandywine and Germantown were discouraging. Even stopping the British advance at Whitemarsh, a victory of sorts, hadn't lifted his spirits, for then all fighting had stopped for the winter. They camped, cold and hungry, at Valley Forge, waiting for a spring that was slow to come.

Thomas stepped around a melting snowdrift. "'Tis true we've not accomplished much this winter," he admitted.

"We've sat around and froze, that's all we've done!"

Patrick said. "If Pa hadn't sent Mary and John along with some pork and turnips, we'd have been livin' on firecake—and like to starved to death."

He held up the ax he was carrying. "We can thank Pa for this, too. The most useful tool we've got." He pointed the ax at a fallen oak tree, lying on its side at the edge of the woods. "We can cut two big branches off that tree. Should give us firewood for a few days."

Thomas nodded, and the cousins took turns with the ax. Wood chips flew into the air and fell on the soggy ground. The late-morning sun slipped behind the thickening clouds. With icy hands, the two boys dragged the branches across the meadow to their small wooden hut, one of many that housed their company.

An hour later, they were inside by the fire. "Is your mind truly made up then about leavin' us in April?" Thomas asked.

"That it is. I see little hope in this starving band of men." Patrick pulled off his boots and wet socks and put his freezing feet as close to the fire as he dared. "I'll do more good helpin' Pa plant the summer crop. And you would, too, cousin."

"Not me," Thomas said, rubbing his hands as the fire warmed them. "I'll not give up our cause."

"Not even if it's a lost one?"

"Not even then. Nor should you. Think, Patrick, of why our fathers came to Pennsylvania. They didn't want us growing up under the yoke of British rule as it is back in Ireland. Sure and you've listened to the same stories I have—about rents and taxes beyond any man's hope of payin'."

"Aye, but . . ."

The wooden door flew open, letting in a cold wind that set the flames dancing and Patrick's feet tingling. It was Sergeant McIntosh. "Patrick O'Connor," he said, "you are to report to the parade ground immediately. Baron von Steuben needs more men for his drill. There aren't enough men in General Washington's honor guard to form a proper company."

"But, sir, I'll not be staying in the army past next month."

"Not according to my orders. See here, it says Patrick O'Connor joined up for two years."

"But I didn't. I just signed on for nine months. There must be a mistake."

"Maybe the sergeant is looking for another Patrick O'Connor," Thomas offered. "There are many O'Connors in Pennsylvania."

"If there are, 'tis of no matter to me," the sergeant said to Thomas. Then he turned to Patrick and said, "You're Patrick O'Connor, and your name is on the list. Now step lively." With that, the sergeant closed the door and was gone.

Thomas looked at Patrick. "Sure and I wish my name was Patrick. I'd be right proud to be in the baron's company. I hear he'll be teachin' marchin' and musket handlin'.

"I handle my musket just fine," Patrick snapped.

But an order must be obeyed. With a sigh, Patrick grabbed some dry rags from his bunk and wrapped them around his still-cold feet. Reluctantly, he pulled on his waterlogged boots. Then he picked up his musket and headed to the parade ground. There he joined a group of soldiers standing in the mud and snow. They all looked older than he, but what a sad-looking group they were—waistcoats tattered, boots bound together with rope, and breeches pieced together like quilts. How could they ever hope to defeat the British army?

A sergeant formed the men into lines just as hoofbeats signaled the arrival of four officers. They promptly dismounted, but only one, a short, heavyset stranger, approached the waiting men.

"I am Baron von Steuben," he said with a heavy foreign accent. "Ve vill learn le march today."

He motioned for a small squad to step forward. "Attention," he said, standing straight and tall. "Attention," he repeated, and pointed to the men in the squad. They stood at attention. Patrick thought they looked fine, but the baron went around correcting each one's position. Finally, he smiled. "Bon," he said, "C'est excellent."

Watching, Patrick was aware of his feet getting colder and colder. How he wished he were back in his hut. Or better yet, back home getting ready for spring planting.

Now the Baron was having the small squad march—forward, halt, about-face, right turn, left turn. Then he divided the entire company into squads, and the drill was done again and again and again.

"Sure as I'm sittin' here, we must've marched from here

to New York," Patrick complained to Thomas when he was finally back at the hut thawing out his frozen feet. "Ah, if only I could find the Patrick O'Connor who's supposed to be doin' this."

After a few more days, Patrick could hear the baron's call in his sleep. "Von, two, tree, four. Von, two, tree, four." He also could hear the Baron's colorful insults when they made mistakes. "Les stupides!" he would roar, or "Dummköpfe!"

One day, they were marching as usual, when the baron called out an order. "Tournez à gauche." Patrick heard "turn" but didn't know which way. He turned right. So did about half the company. The other half turned left.

"Non, non, non!" the baron shouted. "Gauche! Gauche!" Patrick switched directions and turned left, but the men who had turned left, turned right. Soon they were all going in different directions.

The baron threw his hat onto the ground. His face turned red. "Les idiots!" he cried. "Les stupides. Diese Dummköpfe."

Patrick bit his lip to keep from laughing, then noticed that some of the watching officers, too, had big smiles on their faces. Finally, one officer stepped forward.

"I am Captain Benjamin Walker of New York, sir," he said to the baron. "I can translate for you."

" 'Tis almost a shame Captain Walker came forward and straightened everyone out," said Patrick later, chuckling as he told Thomas the story. " 'Twas the first good laugh I was havin' in a long time." Then he added, "But I have to say, the man does know about fightin'. Why just the other day, he showed us a new manual of arms. And I'd swear to it, he can load and fire a musket faster than I ever could. In truth, he's a right good soldier."

"I envy you, cousin," said Thomas. "I'd like to learn the new drill, too."

"And so you shall. Soon the whole army will learn. But here now, I can teach you the manual of arms. You'll need it more than I."

Whenever he wasn't sleeping, eating, or on guard duty, Patrick drilled. Late one afternoon, he was cold, weary, and wet from the driving rain. He took a shortcut through the darkening woods to get back to his hut. The trees were like menacing animals as they swayed in the wind. Suddenly, Patrick realized that two of the "trees" weren't trees at all, but men. He was about to call out a greeting but stopped when he heard a horse neigh. Only officers had horses—and why would an officer be in the woods now? He stepped behind a large bush and peered through its branches.

"Well, now, have we seen enough?" one of the men asked his companion. His neatly trimmed beard seemed out of place with his shabby clothes.

"I would say so, although I don't think General Howe will be happy with our report," said the other.

"No, but 'tis necessary for him to know that the colonials seem well trained and strong," the bearded man replied. "The drill we saw today was most impressive."

Patrick's eyes opened wide. The men were British spies! Without thinking, he stepped back and fell over a tree stump, snapping twigs as he crashed to the ground. Not daring to move, he listened. But the two men had stopped talking.

Now Patrick could hear branches rustling. The men

had heard him. He held his breath. He mustn't be caught. He had heard horrible stories about British prisons, and General Washington must be told that British spies lurked in the woods.

The footsteps came closer. Patrick knew he'd have to move. He took a deep breath, gripped his musket, then sprang to his feet and started running toward camp.

"There!" yelled one of the men. "Catch him."

Footsteps pounded behind Patrick, but he knew these woods better than they did.

"Spies!" he yelled, as he zigzagged through the trees. "Spies on the hill." The footsteps behind him stopped. But Patrick kept running until he reached his camp and Sergeant McIntosh's quarters.

"Spies," he gasped when the sergeant opened the door of his hut. Patrick gulped in air as if he had just remembered to breathe. "British spies in the woods! Right up the hill! We must send men out to find them."

The sergeant touched his shoulder. "Come in, lad, and I will tell you a secret."

They moved close to the fire. "General Washington and his aides know that British spies are about," said Sergeant McIntosh. "But they want them to see the model company and report back to General Howe that our army is strong and disciplined. For now, our orders are to leave them be in the woods."

"But they almost captured me," Patrick protested.

"Aye, but you were a clever lad, and they didn't." The sergeant's blue eyes crinkled in a smile. "The general needs soldiers like you who know what freedom means."

Patrick trudged back to his cabin. The sergeant's last words echoed in his head. Did the general need him? Did he want to fight for freedom? Could they win? He wasn't sure about anything now, but he remembered feeling a surge of pride when the spies had praised the model company's drill. Was that reason enough to stay?

More days of hard drilling still didn't answer his questions. But like the rest of the baron's company, Patrick looked forward to April 6, when they would show off their new skills. When that day came, Patrick put on the shirt he had washed the day before and the new blue waistcoat he had been issued. Then he picked up his musket and headed to the parade ground.

The wind blew raw and cold, but hundreds of soldiers gathered around to watch. Many farmers and their families also came, sitting in wooden wagons around the field. Patrick looked at his fellow soldiers, neatly dressed, standing in straight lines. With the others, Patrick went through the manual of arms, then demonstrated how to march and turn in formation. All the men kept in step as they drilled around the field.

A cheer started in the crowd. Others took it up. "Hurray!" they shouted. "Hurray for our army!" Patrick heard Thomas's voice louder than all the others.

Patrick threw back his shoulders and stood tall. Other soldiers did the same. Yes, he could see it now. They were a real army, and they could win this fight with the British.

Father's fields would have to wait another year for him. He was a soldier with battles to fight.

Did you know . . . that Baron von Steuben was recommended to George Washington by Benjamin Franklin, who was in France in 1777? Historians doubt that von Steuben was really a baron. But he was an expert in military science and knew how to train men. He began with a model company of 150 men, including Washington's squad, then expanded the training to other units. He insisted that officers drill their own men, a new idea to Continental officers, who felt that such work was beneath them. In the British army, with which they were familiar, sergeants, not officers, did the drilling.

Von Steuben emphasized cleanliness and order, and he encouraged officers to get to know their men and win their trust. He gave orders—yelling and swearing—in German, French, and broken English. But he had a good nature, and the men came to like and respect him. Von Steuben also wrote a training manual. He worked with the men during the day and wrote the next day's drill in the evening. Alexander Hamilton, one of Washington's aides, and others translated his manual into English, and then other officers copied it for their brigades.

This newcomer to America stayed with the army until the end of the war and became an American citizen. He loved his new country. During the war, on July 4, 1779, he wrote to a friend in Europe, "What a beautiful, what a happy country this is! Without kings, without prelates, without blood-sucking farmer-generals, and without idle barons. . . . Indeed, I should become too prolix [wordy] were I to give you an account of the prosperity and happiness of these people."

IV
THE REVOLUTION IN THE SOUTH

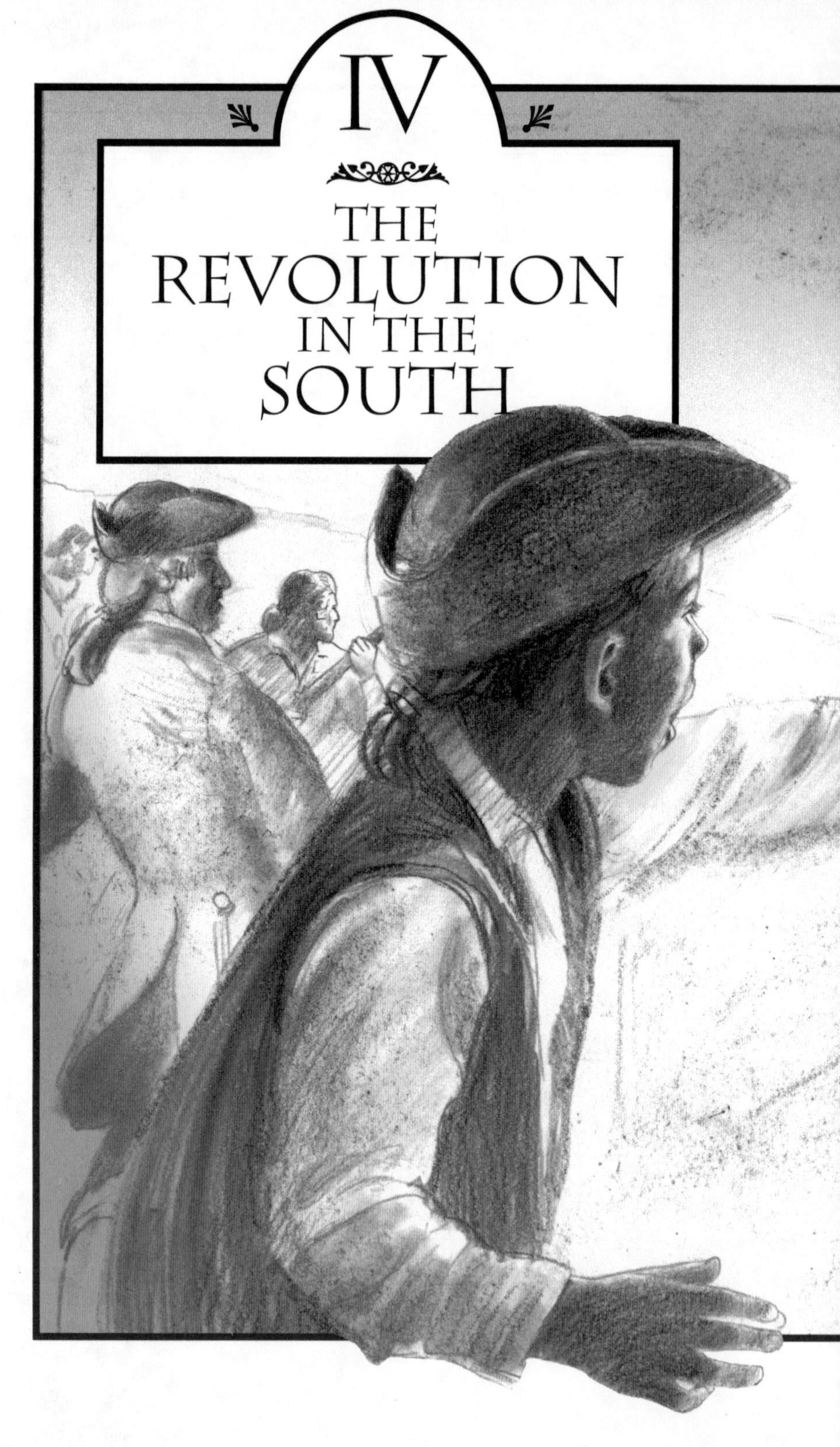

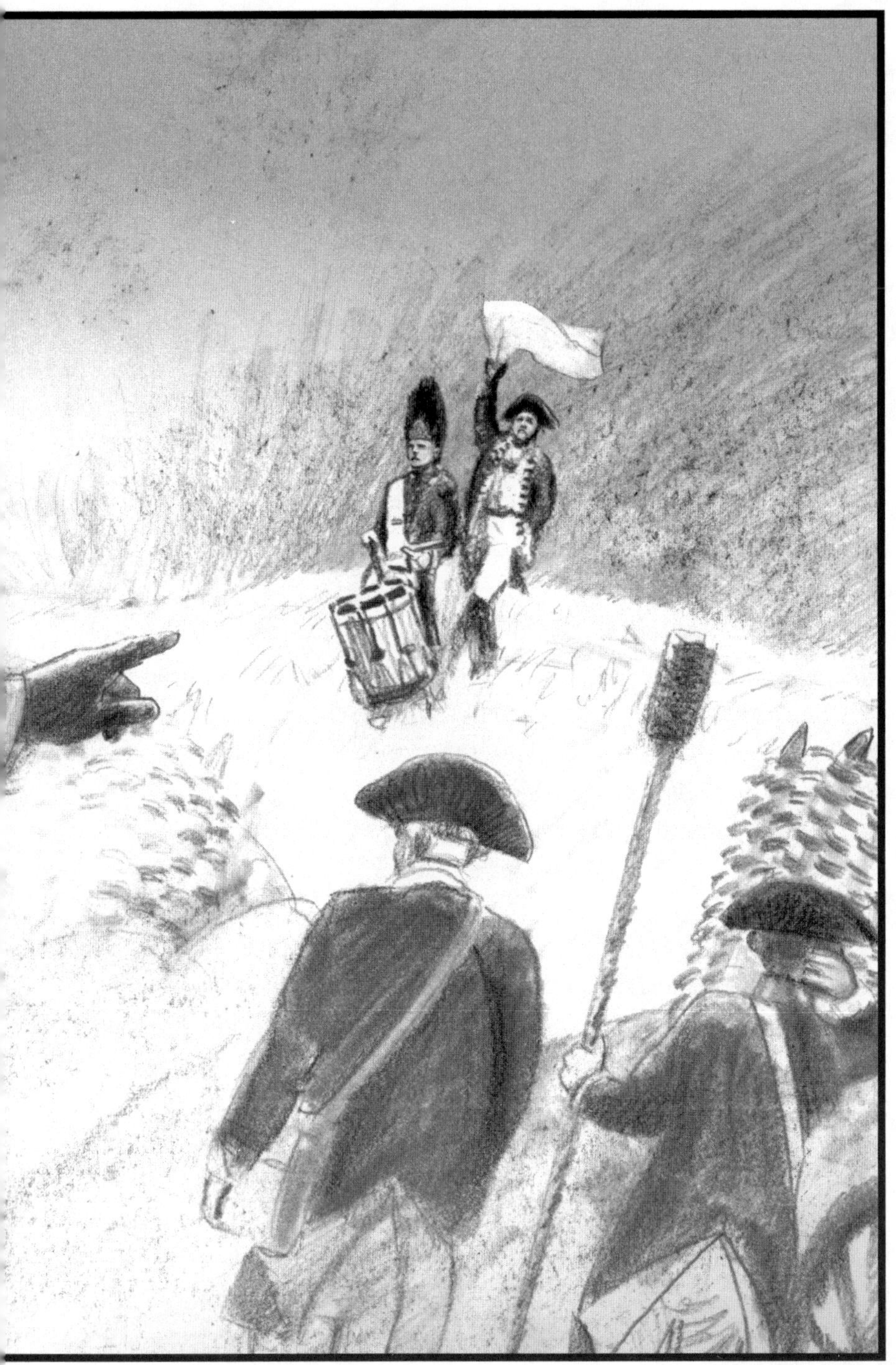

"Thanks Be!" on pages 98–105

A SEDER NIGHT IN CHARLESTON

by Molly Perry

While Washington and his army spent the bitter winter at Valley Forge, the British turned their attention to the colonies in the South. A major plan was to capture southern seaports and stop America's ally—France—from supplying valuable goods to the patriot army.

On December 29, 1778, the British seized the port city of Savannah, Georgia, a victory that encouraged them to push farther inland. Southern Tories disappointed the British by not gathering in large numbers around the royal banner, but the British were still able to expand their control. Finally, the new British commander in chief, Sir Henry Clinton, decided the time was right to march again on Charleston, South Carolina. (Some years earlier, in June 1776, a British attack on the city had been repulsed.)

On February 11, 1780, Clinton put ashore five thousand soldiers thirty miles south of the city and quickly surrounded it on three sides. Soon thereafter, the British fleet blockaded the harbor. The **siege** *of Charleston had begun.*

The American army under General Benjamin Lincoln and the citizens of Charleston held out for several weeks. Finally, on May 12, short of food and ammunition, Lincoln surrendered the city. An entire army—seven generals and six thousand men—was taken prisoner by the British. The surrender of Charleston was a reeling loss for the Americans.

What was it like inside the city during the siege? A young boy named Moses Sheftall lived in Charleston at the time. His father, Mordecai, and his older brother had been taken prisoner by the British in late 1778. Moses and the rest of his family were left to survive as best they could in a city under siege.

MOSES SHEFTALL AND HIS TWO YOUNGER sisters and brother huddled together in front of an upstairs bedroom window. Loud booms of British cannon fire shook the house. In the distance, the children could see the damaged warehouses by the harbor, some only skeletons silhouetted against the afternoon sky. It was April 20, 1780, and the British siege of Charleston had been going on for weeks. It was also the first night of **Passover.**

"Children! Come downstairs now!" Mama called. "I need your helping hands!"

The children ran noisily down the wooden steps to see Mama lifting a lace cloth high into the air over the table as she began to prepare for the Seder meal that night. Passover was Moses' favorite holiday because it was the joyous retelling of the Jewish escape from Egypt and because it included a delicious dinner. He tried to feel his usual

SIEGE—*The encirclement of an army or city by enemy forces. Starvation and/or bombardment are used to force those who are trapped to surrender.*

PASSOVER—*A Jewish commemoration of the Exodus of the ancient Hebrews from enslavement in Egypt. It is celebrated by the Seder, a traditional dinner.*

excitement and block out any thoughts of what had happened the day before. A British cannonball fired from a ship in the harbor had exploded in the street. Mrs. Meyer's daughter Rachel and her nurse were killed walking to market.

Mama carefully smoothed out the tablecloth and lifted her chin with determination. "These are terrible times, but I promised Papa that we would have the Seder, no matter what," she said. "We'll join together with our neighbor Sara and her little Anna."

"What about Daniel?" Moses asked. "Won't he be coming?"

Daniel, Anna's big brother, was twelve. When Moses' older brother had gone with Papa to fight the British, Daniel had become Moses' big brother, too.

"Daniel is working at the hospital," Mama answered. "With so many wounded, they need all the help they can get. Sara said he would try to come."

Moses thought of other years when his family observed Passover in their home in "our beautiful Savannah," as Mama said. He remembered the dining room table, its polished surface set with the hand-painted blue china, silverware, glass Seder plate, and silver wine cups, with a special large cup for the Prophet Elijah.

Now Moses watched Mama place tin plates and mugs on the table, the only tableware they had. The china had been left behind when they had fled Savannah just ahead of the advancing British army. And there would be no roasted egg on the Seder plate to help them remember spring and the continuation of life. During the long British siege of Charleston, most of the hens had already been killed for food.

Moses looked again at the simple table Mama was setting in the living room. If only Papa and his brother were here, he wouldn't care where or how they had their Seder.

Mama took some worn napkins out of the sideboard and turned to Moses again. "I just remembered, Moses, where is the letter you were going to write to Papa? The mail rider is leaving tomorrow. God willing, Papa will receive it even in the British prison."

Moses ran upstairs to Mama and Papa's room and raised the lid of a large wooden trunk. There at the bottom, under some blankets and table linens, were fifteen precious sheets of writing paper that Papa had bought from the stationer in Savannah. Paper was difficult to get in the colonies. Moses knew how fortunate he and Mama were to have even the few sheets left in the trunk. He took one sheet out, folded it once, and put it in his pocket. He would write to Papa in the garden after dinner. Then he went back downstairs to help Mama prepare for the Seder.

When the sun went down, Mama lit the candles to begin Passover. Sara, Anna, Moses, and his younger siblings watched the flickering candlelight dance across Mama's face as she said the blessing.

"This is a celebration of freedom given to us long ago," Mama began. Moses thought about freedom for Papa, his brother, and so many others who were prisoners right now in the colonies. If only they could be free!

Halfway through the Seder meal, there was a soft knock on the door. Moses jumped up and ran to the door, opening it to Daniel.

The older boy slipped into the chair next to Moses. His usually neatly combed hair was tangled, and his brown eyes looked tired as he began eating the dinner that was placed before him. "I can stay for only an hour," he said. "There is much work to be done at the hospital."

After they sang the songs to finish the Seder, Daniel leaned over and whispered, "Moses, please come back to the hospital with me. You can help, too."

"Me?" Moses whispered back. "What could I possibly do?"

"Whatever they tell you! Just come."

"Mama would never let me," Moses said softly to Daniel. And then they realized that Mama was standing behind them.

"It's too dangerous," Mama said, picking up some plates from the table. "The British siege guns fire at any movement inside the city."

Daniel persisted. "But we have many wounded since the British surprise attack at Biggin's Bridge."

"Where our army lost its last escape route!" cried Sara. "Oh, for peace!"

Daniel went on. "I'll keep Moses safe. I have a dark jacket, and so does he. I know all the back ways. We need him, even for only a few hours."

Moses looked at Daniel, then at Mama. "I have to go," he said. "I was too young to go with Papa, but this is something I can do. Please don't say no. I'll be safe." He ran to the door with Daniel, grabbing his dark brown jacket, before Mama had a chance to stop him.

As promised, Daniel got them safely to the back of the

large house that served as a hospital. On an open hearth near some outbuildings, rice steamed in a huge kettle. Suddenly, Moses was afraid to go inside, but he knew he had to follow Daniel.

"Fetch me some more bandages, boy," said a small, tired-looking woman, pointing to a back room.

There sat a very old lady with bright blue eyes, folding bandages from white cloths piled in a large basket. She filled Moses' arms, and he ran up the stairs. He stopped by a writing desk at the top landing and listened to the sounds of men groaning. His feet felt frozen to the floor. He knew he had to take in the bandages, but he couldn't move.

After what seemed like hours, Moses felt a familiar hand on his shoulder. It was Daniel. Gently, he took the bandages. "Come on, Moses, I'll walk in with you."

The room was dimly lit by a few flickering candles, with five beds on either side. In each bed lay a wounded soldier. Two women walked about, quietly taking care of them. Moses looked around. He wanted to run from the suffering. He wanted to run until he got to the safety of home with Mama.

"Hey, boy, come here!" said one of the soldiers in a low, hoarse voice.

Moses looked around and realized that Daniel was gone and the soldier was speaking to him.

He hesitated. "I'll talk to him for a minute," he said to himself, "and then run straight home."

Moses took three slow steps toward the bed. Bloodied bandages covered the man's right eye and bound his right arm to his body. He reached out with his left arm and took

Moses' hand. Moses swallowed hard, resisting the desire to pull his hand free.

"You look like my boy William," the man said. "What's your name?"

"Moses Sheftall, sir." His mouth was dry, like dusty cotton.

"My name is Andrew Thompson, Corporal Andrew Thompson. Now sit with me a while, would ye, Moses?"

Moses sat down, turning his eyes away from the bandages and looking longingly at the door. Corporal Thompson began to talk to Moses like a long-lost friend. He told Moses about his farm a few miles south of Charleston, about how his wife liked to sing while she worked in the kitchen or when she put the children to bed. The more Moses listened to Corporal Thompson, the more the soldier reminded him of Papa. Moses knew how sad Corporal Thompson was because he missed Papa and his brother just as much.

The soldier smiled, still holding Moses' hand. But now, somehow, Moses didn't mind.

"I wish I could tell my family where I am and not to worry about me," Corporal Thompson said more to himself than to Moses.

But Moses heard, and he had an idea. He pulled free of the corporal's hand. "I'll be right back," he said. He hurried to the landing, where he took out a small glass inkwell and a quill pen from the writing desk. Carefully, he drew the sheet of paper from his pocket. He had more paper at home to write to Papa.

This time, he did not freeze before entering the room. He walked straight over to Corporal Thompson.

"Sir," Moses whispered.

"Good to see you again, boy." The soldier winced in pain as he tried to move his head.

"I can write a letter to your wife and children for you."

"I'm mighty obliged to you, Moses," said the corporal.

For a long time, Moses carefully wrote the words that Corporal Thompson dictated to him. As he folded the finished letter, he could almost hear Papa's voice in his ear. Papa had said to him many times, "It is written that to save a single life is like saving the whole world. Remember this always, Moses."

"Well, Papa," Moses whispered, "today I've helped a life. And perhaps someday I will save a life."

He went downstairs to find Daniel. "I'm leaving now," he said. "Mama will be worried. I can go home alone."

As he walked through the dark streets, Moses heard a hissing sound. A cat exploring the night? Another hiss, and suddenly two figures—one larger than Moses and the other thin and small—blocked his way. Moses recognized them as Tories.

"What have we here?" rasped one. "A young patriot out and about. What are you doing out at this time of night?"

"I've been working at the hospital helping with the wounded."

"Think you're brave, don't you? Your father isn't. Or else he would have escaped the prison ship when the others did, by swimming Musgrove Creek."

"My father is a prisoner with my brother, who cannot swim. Father would never leave him behind."

The two boys drew closer. "Perhaps," said the larger boy,

"we should find out if our patriot friend *here* can swim. A toss in Charleston Harbor would prove it."

"Close to the British ships would be even better," added the smaller one with a chuckle.

Swiftly, the boys grabbed Moses' arms, pinning them behind his back. Moses tore one arm free, but the boys seized it again. Before they had a chance to bind his wrists, Moses flung himself forward. The small boy lost his balance, and Moses struck the other one in the stomach. In the brief moment of surprise, he slipped out of their grasp and ran hard, dodging in and out of the shadows.

Moses raced down Church Street past the bookbinder's shop and the assembly hall, where he had often heard the rising and falling voices of slave auctioneers. Flowering jasmine from the garden of a Tory family that had fled to England filled the air with a sickening sweetness. Moses felt cold. The bells of St. Michael's Church tolled ten.

Finally reaching home, he paused by the gate and listened for footsteps. None came. Then he went inside the house, leaning against the parlor door to catch his breath. He could hear his mother's voice coming from Sara's house next door. He would never tell her what had happened, for he wanted more than anything to return to the hospital. But next time, he would take a safer and faster route home.

Upstairs, Moses lit a candle. Carefully, he took another sheet of paper from the trunk. He began to write. "Dear Papa, this Seder night was truly different from all others—and an important one for me."

Did you know . . . that after the Americans surrendered Charleston, the British seized three wealthy residents, all signers of the Declaration of Independence? Thomas Heyward, Jr., Edward Rutledge, and Arthur Middleton were marched out of the city and taken to St. Augustine, Florida—which was still loyal to Britain—and held under guard until the war's end.

Do you wonder . . . what happened to Moses Sheftall? Early in 1781, the British moved his father and brother to Philadelphia, where they were freed in a prisoner exchange. Moses and his family managed to join them there. After the war, Moses stayed in Philadelphia to study medicine with Dr. Benjamin Rush, a patriot and prominent physician. When Moses completed his studies, he returned to Savannah, where he practiced medicine.

Charleston, 1780

WILLIAM'S WAR

by Elizabeth Weiss Vollstadt

After the defeat at Charleston in May 1780, the war in the South looked grim for the patriots. They lost battle after battle, fighting not only British troops but also Loyalist neighbors. The patriots continued their struggle, however, forming guerrilla bands to harass the British army. They attacked communication and supply lines and then escaped into the forests and swamps they knew so well.

But the British hold over the southern colonies grew stronger, and they decided it was time to put down the rebellion once and for all. They declared that anyone who refused to serve in the king's militia would be put in prison and his property taken. In addition, any former militiamen who had signed statements saying they would not fight again and then had joined the ***guerrillas*** *would be executed without a trial if captured. Farms were destroyed, homes burned, and men killed as these orders were carried out, often by Loyalists who supported the king.*

British major Patrick Ferguson successfully organized a Loyalist militia of approximately one thousand men and tried to gain the support of the people of the Carolinas. He made a mistake, however, when he threatened the independent pioneers in the mountains of what are now western North and South Carolina, eastern Tennessee, and southwestern Virginia. He sent word that if

GUERRILLAS—*Unofficial military groups operating in small bands to sabotage the enemy.*

they didn't stop resisting British rule, he would march his army over the mountains and "lay waste the country with fire and sword."

His words were a call to action to these mountain men. They were not going to wait for trouble to come to them; they would find it first. At the end of September 1780, bands of frontiersmen marched over the mountains in pursuit of Ferguson. These "over-mountain men," as they came to be called, found him on October 7 at Kings Mountain, a high ridge just over the border in South Carolina, about thirty miles southwest of Charlotte, North Carolina.

Neighbor turned against neighbor, as old feuds were renewed and new anger unleashed. Like their parents, young people were caught in the struggle.

WILLIAM WATCHED THE ORANGE FLAMES blaze higher and higher around his family's cabin. Wood crackled as the flames devoured the dry logs, until they collapsed in a fiery heap. Sparks showered the yard. The barn burned, too, an unnatural brightness lighting up the North Carolina sky. He could hear his mother sobbing as she watched everything they had—benches, table, chairs, bedding, clothing, cooking utensils, and, most important, food—disappear in the raging fire.

Although the night was cool, sweat poured from William's body as he shook with fear and fury. "No!" he screamed. "No!"

"William. William. Wake up! Thee is having another nightmare."

He opened his eyes. The fire was gone. He lay safely in

bed at his uncle's home. His mother was leaning over him.

"It was the fire," William said. "It's always the fire. How could they do that to us? I even recognized Mr. McBride!"

William couldn't understand how their Loyalist neighbors could burn down their farm, just because his father supported the rebels. Mr. McBride and Pa used to share supplies before the war started. And fifteen-year-old Daniel McBride, just a year older than William, had been William's best friend. William couldn't forget Mr. McBride's angry face as he threw a lighted torch into their barn. Over and over, the fire came back in his dreams, making him relive that terrible night.

His mother sat down on the bed that William shared with his little brother, Eli, who lay quietly, still deep in sleep. "I don't know, son," she said, her face creased with sadness. "But war does awful things to people. This war of ours for independence has been going on for five years now. I pray it ends before there are no civilized folks left—and before it's too late for forgiveness."

"It's already too late," William said bitterly. "I'll never forgive those Loyalists. Not if I live a thousand years!"

"Oh, William, thee must not harbor such hatred in thy heart."

William said nothing. He knew that his mother, born a Quaker, supported the patriot cause, but she believed that they should look for a peaceful solution.

Last year, running through the woods with Daniel, William could agree with her. But no more. All he wanted now was revenge for what the Loyalists, especially Daniel's father, had done to them.

William's mother sighed and smoothed the quilt around him. "Try to get some sleep now," she said. "We're safe here in Uncle Thomas's mountains. The war is far away."

But that night at dinner, news from Uncle Thomas brought the war closer. "Looks like trouble's brewin' again," he said to Pa. "Neighbor came by this afternoon. Seems like those British won't let folks live in peace. That Major Ferguson is stirrin' things up. It's not enough that his Loyalist traitors are settin' neighbor against neighbor. Now he's sent word that if we don't stop our opposition to the king, he'll march his army over our mountains, hang our leaders, and destroy our country with fire and sword. Them's his very words, I hear, 'with fire and sword.' "

William's heart almost stopped at the word *fire.* No! It couldn't happen again! He wouldn't let it. Anger against the Loyalists rose in his throat, almost choking him. They had to be stopped.

Pa echoed his thoughts. "I hate that man Ferguson. If I found him, he'd not walk away alive."

"Thee must not talk like that," Ma protested. "We are to forgive—"

"Hush," said Pa. "Let others forgive. I'll not watch another farm go up in flames." He turned back to Uncle Thomas. "What do your neighbors say?"

"Same as you," Uncle Thomas said. "This has gone far enough. We must keep them away from our homes."

Word spread swiftly to the surrounding farms. By the following evening, the mountain men had made their plans. They would join other patriot militiamen to find Ferguson. Then they would destroy him before he and his men could destroy them.

Faces were grim around the dinner table as Pa and Uncle Thomas made their plans.

"I want to go with you," William said, shoving back his chair to stand up and face the two men. "I've got a rifle, and I can shoot. You know I can, Pa. You've always said I'm the best shot in the family."

Before his pa could answer, William's mother said, "No. I cannot stop thy father, but thee is still young enough. I'll not have all my men off gettin' themselves killed."

His pa nodded. "Your ma and I don't see eye to eye on this war, but she is right about this. You're too young. You stay here and help your ma and aunt Sarah with the farm and the younger children."

"We don't need lookin' after," said Eli, sitting up straight.

"'Tis no matter," said William's mother, smiling at her young son. "William is staying here."

William held back a protest that they weren't being fair. It was his home that had been burned. He wanted to do something—no, he *had* to do something.

A few days later, in the predawn darkness, William watched his father and uncle ride off. They didn't know it, but he would not be left behind. He had already written a short note to Ma and left it on his pillow. He slipped out of the house and headed to the barn.

Clutched tightly in his hands was his rifle. In his breeches pocket was a piece of bread saved from the previous night's dinner. He opened the barn door and led his horse out into the woods. Thank the Lord that he and

Pa had been able to save the horses from the burning barn. Now he would follow the men in secret until night, when he would appear at their camp. By then, it would be too late to send him back.

It was cool for September, and William pulled his deerskin shirt tightly around him. When the sun was high, he ate his bread and stopped briefly at a stream to drink and water his horse. A startled white-tailed deer leaped for cover. Dry fallen leaves crackled and branches snapped under his horse's hooves. At times, William was sure the men would hear him. Then he would stop and keep very still.

Finally, the men stopped to make camp for the night. William waited until he saw a fire blazing and smelled smoked pork cooking.

Tying his horse to a tree, he walked into the camp. Suddenly, he was looking at two rifles, and they were pointed at him.

"Wait!" he said. "I'm a friend! My name's William McNabb. My pa and uncle Thomas are with you . . . I swear . . ."

The rifles didn't move. William's knees started to tremble, and he forgot to breathe. Then he heard his father's voice. "Put down those rifles. Can't you tell a boy when you see one? This is my son William, and he's just fourteen."

"Well, I'll be," said one of the men, as he lowered his rifle. "But we can't be too careful."

"It ain't too smart to be sneakin' up on folks in these parts, boy," said the other.

They walked away, leaving William to face his father. "Explain yourself, son," he said, his face clouded with anger. "What are you doing here? I told you to stay at the farm."

"I had to come, Pa. The fire—it's eatin' at me all the time. I have to fight. It's all I can think of."

"I should give you a good whippin' and send you back," his pa said. He looked at the dark woods. "But I guess you'll be safer with us. You'll have to keep up, though. And when we do battle, I'll need your word that you'll stay behind. I owe your mother that. You must swear an oath."

"But I want . . . ," William protested. His anger at the Loyalists made his voice shake.

"You have already disobeyed me once. Now swear your oath." The look on Pa's face told William he would hear no argument.

"All right," William said. "I swear that I'll stay behind when a battle begins."

The next few days were long and hard as they followed Ferguson's army through the Carolina woods. Finally, they learned from spies that Ferguson and his Loyalist followers were making a stand on a high ridge called Kings Mountain. They joined forces with Colonel William Campbell and his army of nine hundred men. Despite the rain that fell that October day, William felt only excitement as they hurried toward the ridge.

Shortly before 3:00 P.M., they arrived, wet and cold, at the foot of Kings Mountain. The rain had stopped, but the maple and chestnut trees still showered them with drops.

"Remember your oath," said William's father. "You stay down here and help take care of our horses and supplies."

The assault started. William could hear the sound of rifles and the whooping of the men as they slowly inched their way up the mountain. One hour passed. The whooping stopped, but the gunfire continued. Finally, the guns were still. All William could hear was shouting and cries from the wounded.

"What's happening?" he asked one of the men guarding the horses with him.

"Don't know, lad. Scout around and see what you can find out. But don't go too far. I'll not have any harm comin' to ye."

William moved slowly through the forest, the tall oak and maple trees still glistening with raindrops. He climbed a little way up the mountain and peered through a clearing. But he couldn't see the plateau above the rise. Suddenly, a figure came flying out of a stand of trees, charging down the mountain toward him. William grabbed his rifle. At last, he would be part of the war.

"Halt," he shouted, "or I'll shoot!"

The figure stumbled over a fallen log and stopped. William looked at him. He blinked. No, it couldn't be. Daniel McBride, his old friend, stood before him, his torn clothes covered with mud. He was breathing hard, eyes wide with fear. Then he recognized William.

"William," he said, "don't shoot. It's me, Daniel, remember?" Some of the fear left his eyes.

"I remember all right," William said. "I remember your pa burnin' down our barn. And now you've joined him. I won't shoot. But I'm takin' you prisoner."

The fear returned to Daniel's eyes. "Please, William. I . . . I can't stand any more. It's horrible up there. I must get home. Pa's been killed—and so many others. Even Major Ferguson. Your side's won. Ain't that enough?"

"No. Why should I care about your gettin' home? Thanks to your pa and his friends, I don't even have a home."

"I'm right sorry about that," Daniel said, "and Ma was, too. She liked your ma and your family. Please, just let me go. Ma will need me. I'll head right home. I'm finished with this war."

William looked at Daniel's face, heard the pleading in his voice. This was his chance to get his revenge. But then he saw himself and Daniel, jumping into the river in the summer, hunting together in the fall, throwing snowballs in the winter, helping each other with planting in the spring. And Daniel's mention of William's mother brought back her words about the war: "I pray it ends before there are no civilized folks left—and before it's too late for forgiveness."

They were civilized folks, he and his family. His hate and anger slowly dissolved. Daniel had lost his father. That was enough. William wasn't ready to forgive, but he would let Daniel go home.

"Go on," he finally said, pointing east with his rifle. Then he shouted, "Wait! Did you see my pa?"

"I'm not right sure, but I saw someone that looked mighty like him."

The two boys looked at each other once more, then at William's nod, Daniel slipped into the woods and was gone.

William watched him disappear, then set off in the opposite direction. Someday, he thought, when this long war is over, maybe he could go home, too, to rebuild the farm. And maybe by then he could forgive. He hoped that Daniel was right and that Pa—and Uncle Thomas—had survived the battle. He quickened his pace. Back at the horses, he would wait for news.

Did you know . . . that the Battle of Kings Mountain was very important to the American cause? It is considered to be the turning point of the Revolution in the South. It shook the confidence of the British, who had counted on Ferguson to put down all opposition in the Carolinas and Virginia. It also revived the hopes of the patriots. Guerrilla fighters stepped up their harassment of British troops. Patriot supporters increased their attacks on their Loyalist neighbors. And the next big battle, the Battle of Cowpens, would end in another patriot victory. The stage was being set for the all-important siege at Yorktown.

The Battle of Cowpens

THANKS BE!

by Marcella Fisher Anderson

The Battle of Kings Mountain in October 1780 was followed by the Battle of Cowpens, also in South Carolina, on January 17, 1781. The fighting at Guilford Courthouse, North Carolina, on March 15, 1781, caused some high-ranking British officers to become discouraged about their prospects for success in the southern colonies. British general Henry Clinton and his second in command, General Charles Cornwallis, disagreed on basic strategy.

Without consulting Clinton, Cornwallis moved his army in May from North Carolina to Virginia, where he tried unsuccessfully to bring the state under British control. In early August, he reached the York River, which flows into the Chesapeake Bay. He stopped at a tobacco port named Yorktown, where his army made camp and started to build fortifications. Cornwallis believed that the Yorktown location would ensure support from British ships.

But on September 5, the French and British fleets met off the Virginia coast in the Battle of the Virginia Capes. When the sea battle ended, the French controlled the waters off Yorktown. The British sailed lamely to New York for extensive repairs to their ships.

Meanwhile, Clinton, in New York City, prepared for an expected combined attack by Washington's troops and the French navy under Admiral François Joseph Paul de Grasse. Toward the end of August, Clinton refused to believe reliable reports that Washington's army, de Grasse's ships, and French general Jean

Baptiste de Rochambeau's troops were all converging on Yorktown. Cornwallis's outnumbered force was soon under siege—a siege that would last for three weeks, from September 28 to October 19.

Despite these events, life in the colonies moved determinedly on, often centered on the tavern, where people gathered to eat, drink, play games, and share the news of the day. Children helped harvest the crops and threw the last stones of summer into nearby ponds. Some young people strayed farther from home, as this story illustrates.

BEN PUSHED ASIDE THE SALT GRASS that was almost as tall as he was. The October sun was rising over the York River. To the north, smoke from the British army's breakfast fires drifted above the Yorktown encampment. Recognizing loud rumblings from the south, Ben knew that the Americans and French were positioning heavy guns for another bombardment.

He hurried to the river, thinking about the flounder he would catch for the supper menu at his aunt's tavern on the road to Williamsburg. He wondered whether Rodney, a young British drummer he had met one day at water's edge, would be waiting for him. He imagined Rodney's eyes crinkling in a smile as he spoke: "I say, Ben, knew ya'd come. Time ta take the boat out." But when Ben reached the water's edge, a cut rope lay at his feet, and his boat—always tied to the willow—was gone.

Ben shaded his eyes. Not far up the river, he spotted his dory stranded on a sandbar and someone in a British uniform standing up in it, pushing off with an oar. "Stop!"

Ben shouted. "That's my boat!"

As Ben got closer, he recognized the boatman: it was the drummer. "Rodney, what are you doing? I thought we were friends," he said. A cold finger of betrayal crossed Ben's heart. "Didn't I trust you? I taught you how to trap rabbits and catch flounder and keep it fresh in the sand, didn't I?"

Rodney didn't respond. Fiercely now, his gangling frame bent to the task, Rodney worked the boat free and rowed rapidly toward the encampment.

Ben stared, then began running again. Around a bend, he saw that other stolen craft were clustered at the river's entrance. A portly British officer stood ordering the boats ashore.

Ben ducked down in the grass. He sat on the bank, arms clasped around his trembling knees. He knew that the wind had blown his words away. For Rodney's sake, he was grateful that Rodney hadn't been caught befriending an American. Ben had heard that British army discipline was swift and cruel for anyone who spoke with the enemy or slipped away from camp: fifty lashes, at least, with a cat-o'-nine-tails whip.

In a mood as heavy as the clouds darkening the sky, Ben returned empty-handed to the tavern where he lived with his aunt Martha. For supper, he picked carrots and onions from the garden, added water to the cabbage soup, and served the few customers. A gusting wind blew through the door each time it was opened. Before he went to bed, he latched the casement windows.

Ben awoke to a bombardment that shook the smoke-blackened walls and rattled Aunt Martha's best china. He hurried into the taproom just as two customers came in for breakfast. Their Continental army coats were tattered and frayed.

One man pressed a damp cloth to his forehead; a black patch covered one eye. "Worst shelling I've ever heard," he said hoarsely.

"Tried to escape the siege lines last night, the British did," said the other man. "Crossed the York River to Gloucester Point." Limping, he pulled back a chair. "A squall caught them. Most of the boats were scattered. Only a few are back now. Baked eggs and cider, if you please."

Ben rushed through his work and left before his aunt could think of more chores for him to do. He ran toward the American siege lines, tearing through fields of goldenrod. Panicked quail fled toward him. Distant bells rang ten o'clock.

Out on the York River, the topsails of the French ships stretched across the water. The British were in a box and couldn't escape. Ben could see that.

He squinted, focusing his eyes on the battered British fortifications. Suddenly, a British drummer stood on top of a wall. Ben ran closer. The boom of cannon shook the sandy ground beneath his feet. A British ensign held up a large white cloth, waved it above his head, and walked down the embankment, following the drummer. Was it Rodney beating the drum? In a minute, Ben was sure of it. He recognized the lanky build, the sunburned face.

The American and French gunners kept up their steady, accurate fire. Afraid for Rodney, Ben cried, "Stop! Stop firing!"

Steadily, Rodney and the officer walked closer to the American lines, moving in and out of the billowing smoke.

Then, the British ensign's flag seen at last, the

cannonading stopped. A light breeze wafted the smoke away. An American officer walked forward to meet them. Rodney had stopped drumming and held the sticks stiffly at his side. As if in a dream, Ben watched the British officer and Rodney vanish into the American headquarters.

Minutes later, without even remembering having run, he burst into the tavern. "Flag of truce!" he shouted. "Flag of truce!"

An old man standing by the hearth turned around and dropped his clay pipe. "Say that again, lad," he demanded.

"They're meeting right now. In American headquarters." Ben's voice croaked. "I've seen them."

The room was silent. "Listen," said the man with the eye patch. "The guns have stopped."

Aunt Martha set down a pot of oyster stew. She covered her mouth, then clasped her hands together. "Thanks be to God," she said. "Thanks be!"

At once, the men stood up. They swept aside their pewter mugs, sending them clattering in all directions. The tavern emptied.

During the hours that followed, Ben was too busy serving happy and cheering customers to think much about the American victory. But two days later, on the afternoon of the formal surrender proceedings, he walked to Yorktown with Aunt Martha. Ben noted that she had pinned two yellow garden dahlias to her shawl.

Later, Ben smiled as he remembered the British rifles stacked high against the sky and the British effort to save face by trying to present the surrender sword to the French instead of the Americans. Then Ben caught sight of

Rodney, marching off to prison, beating a doleful surrender on his drum, averting his eyes as he passed by.

It was a long and lonely week before Ben went back to the river. Only a few bald eagles soared above. In the early-morning light, he followed a newly broken trail through the tall grass. When he parted it, he gasped at seeing his boat tied to the willow. He peered inside. Two drumsticks lay on the bottom. Rodney! Could he have escaped while on the march to prison?

Ben grinned. Rodney was good at that. Perhaps he had escaped to live off the land as Ben had taught him—until he could become a farmer or shopkeeper. He could almost hear Rodney say again, "There's nothin' fer me in England, and I 'ate the British army, I do. I'm stayin' 'ere ta be a new American." His blue eyes darkened as he added, "Bloody well see if I don't."

Now, spotting a branch stuck upright in a mound of sand, Ben dug into it to uncover a flounder, newly caught and buried on the cool shore. He rinsed the fish in the river. The morning light shone on the scales. And Ben, holding Rodney's flounder aloft, laughed out loud.

Did you know . . . that George Washington's composure prevented the British surrender at Yorktown from becoming a fiasco? A humiliated Cornwallis sent word that he was ill and could not attend the ceremony. He ordered his second in command, General Charles O'Hara, to represent him. Initially, O'Hara tried to present the surrender sword to General Rochambeau. The French commander declined, saying something to the effect that this was America's war. When O'Hara walked toward the American commander in chief, Washington refused to accept the surrender from a British officer lower in military rank than himself. Washington then indicated that O'Hara should present the sword to his second in command, General Benjamin Lincoln. (Lincoln had been freed in a prisoner exchange after having surrendered at Charleston.)

The surrender at Yorktown

Do you wonder . . . what would have happened if Washington's army, Rochambeau's troops, and de Grasse's ships had not all met at Yorktown? If the other troops hadn't arrived, the French fleet would have sailed to the West Indies after only three days. Instead, close communication and coordination resulted in Cornwallis's defeat. Yorktown was one of the Continental army's few clear victories and, for all practical purposes, ended the war.

And what happened to General Clinton? Finally, he set sail for Yorktown on the very day that Cornwallis surrendered. When he reached the Virginia coast, he was met by two British soldiers in small boats. They informed him of the disastrous defeat.

General Henry Clinton

V

A NEW COUNTRY IS BORN

"Learning from the President" on pages 126–133

NEW DAY IN SAVANNAH

by Elizabeth Weiss Vollstadt

Even though the British army surrendered at Yorktown, peace did not come right away. Neither did the British presence in the American colonies end immediately. In the South, the British continued to control Charleston, South Carolina, and Savannah, Georgia, and they showed no signs of leaving.

A few months after Yorktown, the Continental army's commander in the South, General Nathanael Greene, sent General Anthony Wayne to help liberate Georgia. Wayne took back the cities of Augusta, Ebenezer, and Midway before arriving near Savannah in late January 1782. Once there, he encircled the city and waited. The people of Savannah and the surrounding countryside—both patriots and Loyalists—waited, too.

In April, informal peace talks began in Paris. Summer came, and the British Parliament ordered Governor James Wright of Savannah to evacuate the city, leaving it to the rebels. The Loyalists, many of them **plantation** *owners, left their flourishing rice fields and elegant homes and withdrew to Tybee Island, seventeen miles downriver from Savannah, to await the ships that would take them to England. On July 11, 1782, the American army entered Savannah.*

Some Loyalists were probably glad to return to the mother country after so many years of war. Others must have found it hard to leave their plantations and businesses, where they had lived and worked for many years. Many families were split by patriot and Loyalist sentiments. For them, the evacuation meant a permanent separation, as some members returned to England and others stayed in America.

The conflict between father and son in this story is representative of what occurred in many families, as well as between neighbors and friends, during and after the Revolution.

"SWEAR IT," BEN SAID FIERCELY. "Swear your allegiance to the king." He sat on Nathaniel's chest, pinning his arms to the floor.

Nathaniel struggled to break free, but at thirteen, he was no match for his sixteen-year-old brother. Still, he wouldn't give in.

"Never," he gasped. "Old George is not my king. Not anymore." He twisted to the right. Caught off balance, Ben lost his grip. Nathaniel jerked his arms free, turned, and leaped to his feet.

"You and Father don't want to see it, but it's true," he said. He stood with his back against the painted paneled

PLANTATION—*A large farm or estate on which crops are grown, often by workers who live on the plantation. In the colonial South, plantations were made possible by slave labor, which allowed one person or family to cultivate several hundred acres or more. Rice was the main crop in Savannah. By the beginning of the American Revolution, there were about fourteen hundred rice plantations in the area, with an average size of 850 acres.*

wall of the parlor. "The war was over when the redcoats surrendered at Yorktown. Now General Wayne is getting ready to free Savannah. We're going to be a new country!"

"Not Savannah," said Ben. "Savannah will never surrender to the rebels." But he made no move to fight with his brother again. Instead, he said softly, "You'd better hold your tongue. Father does not like to hear such talk. You might get away from me, but if father wants to give you a thrashing, he will."

Nathaniel knew that all too well. During most of the war for independence, Savannah had been occupied and controlled by the British army. His father had been born in England and, like many wealthy plantation owners, had no wish to separate from the mother country. Ben sided with his father.

But not Nathaniel. He was closer to his mother, who had been born in this new land. He never forgot the day she had taken him to hear the Declaration of Independence read at Savannah's Reynolds Square. It was six years ago, but he still remembered the cheers and his mother's words: "Someday, Nathaniel, this will be a new country, where men can make their own laws."

He never spoke of that day at home anymore, not since his mother had died of fever two years before. He knew what defending the patriots would bring. "Hold your tongue, lad!" his father would say, sometimes following his words with a sharp slap.

So Nathaniel would sneak over to the adjoining McInnis plantation, where his friend James lived. The McInnises were dedicated patriots. Nathaniel didn't have to hold his tongue there. He and James could talk about the war for independence and cheer for each colonial victory. James's father would always nod and say, "Well said, boys. We have to get those foreigners off our soil. And we will someday. Then Savannah will be free."

Now Nathaniel needed to hear those cheering words again. He turned away from Ben and escaped to the wide porch that shaded the front of the big plantation house. He had just enough time to see James before dinner. Maybe there was news about when General Wayne would arrive. But just then, his father bounded up the steps, frowning and muttering to himself. Nathaniel heard snatches of "scoundrels . . . never thought it would come to this" before his father saw him and stopped.

"Nathaniel," he said, "come inside. I have word from the governor. We must make plans to leave Savannah."

"Leave Savannah? But why? Where will we go?"

"Home," his father said. "Home to England. Now come."

Nathaniel slowly followed his father back to the parlor. "Governor Wright has been ordered to vacate the city and leave it to the rebels," his father was saying to Ben. "All those loyal to the crown will be given safe passage to England."

He looked at his sons. "We will take whatever we can carry and sail down the river to Tybee Island. The British fleet will pick us up there." For the first time, he smiled. "Ah, it will be good to see old England again. And you lads, I will send you to the finest schools. You will no longer be ignorant colonials."

"How long will the voyage be?" asked Ben. His brown eyes were wide with excitement. He had listened well to his father's tales of life on a big estate in England. "Will we get to see London? Where are the fine schools?"

Nathaniel said nothing. Leave Savannah? Leave Georgia? Impossible! He could see the rice fields and surrounding marshes through the long parlor windows. An egret took flight, soaring above the grasses. Just beyond was the Savannah River, where he and James cooled off during the long, hot summers. And on the hill behind the house was his mother's grave. Nathaniel's heart still ached from missing her, and he visited her grave often. No, he couldn't leave.

But how could he stay?

His father broke into Nathaniel's thoughts. "And you, lad, have you nothing to say?"

"I don't want to go," Nathaniel blurted out. "This is my home."

"But England will be home, too," said Ben. "And what an adventure to sail across the ocean!"

But to Nathaniel, the real adventure would be to own a successful plantation in a new country. "I don't care," he said. "I want—"

"It is of no matter what you want," his father said sternly. "You are my son. You are coming with me." His voice softened. "You will become a fine English gentleman, Nathaniel. You'll see."

Nathaniel tried again. "But what about the plantation?"

"Do you think the rebels will let us keep the plantation, knowing we were loyal to the king?" his father answered.

"Not likely, from what I have heard. No, this is the best we can do. We are lucky to escape with our lives—and with our house servants. Now look to your belongings. We will leave on the morning tide."

He strode out of the room. Ben followed, peppering his father with questions about England. Nathaniel walked onto the porch and sat down on the steps. Although it was late afternoon, the summer sun still hung high in the sky. Everything was hushed in the heat. He breathed in the damp scent of earth and pine from the nearby forest. He could not leave this place. He *would* not. He didn't believe they would lose the plantation. After all, *he* was a patriot.

Dinner stretched on forever. Nathaniel pushed the shrimp and rice around his plate. Every word his father said made the knot in his stomach tighter. Who cared about fancy carriages and castles when they could have salt marshes and rice fields and tall oaks for climbing? His mind skipped from one escape plan to another.

Finally, the two boys were sent upstairs to pack. Nathaniel followed Ben to their large room at the top of the stairs. He would pack, but not for England. He would go to James's father and offer to serve his plantation. He knew more about rice production than many grown men.

Nathaniel told Ben he was going to visit their mother's grave once more and slipped quietly out of the house. The setting sun gave the large oak trees, draped with Spanish moss, a golden glow. A whippoorwill called as Nathaniel neared the McInnis plantation.

"Why, Nathaniel," said Mr. McInnis, who was standing on the porch of his large plantation house, "what brings you here so late? No matter. Come in. We have news. A messenger has just left." He opened the front door, shouting inside, "James, look who's here."

Nathaniel felt the man's warm hand on his shoulder as they entered the familiar parlor. "Nathaniel," cried James, leaping to his feet, "we've just heard! The patriots will enter Savannah tomorrow! The war is really over! And we'll be rid of those wicked Tories, too. They're heading . . ."

"Back to England," Nathaniel interrupted. "I know. My father is among them." His voice was flat, holding none of James's excitement.

James had been heading toward Nathaniel but stopped in his tracks. "Surely your father's not leaving! I know he's a Tory, but how can he? Who will stay here with you and Ben?" He paused. "Oh, no, he doesn't mean to take you, does he? Why, you can't leave! And he can't make you." James turned to his father, who still stood in the doorway, his hand on Nathaniel's shoulder. "Can he, Father?"

Mr. McInnis sighed. "I'm afraid he can."

Nathaniel stepped away from Mr. McInnis. He looked into the man's eyes. "That is why I have come, sir," he said. He pulled himself up as tall as he could. "I wish to offer my services to your plantation. I can work in the rice fields or oversee the workers in the mill. I have learned much from my father."

Mr. McInnis smiled. "Nathaniel, I would be happy to take you into my family, but not as a worker—as a son. But your father is your father. You are under his authority."

"Then I'll run away," said Nathaniel. "I'll . . . I'll join the army, that's what—"

Thump, thump! Someone was pounding on the door. Then, "Open up, McInnis! I know my son is in there. I'll have you charged with kidnapping!"

"It's my father!" Nathaniel gasped.

Mr. McInnis opened the door. "Please come . . . ," he said, as Nathaniel's father stalked into the room. The angry man grabbed Nathaniel by the shoulder.

"No talk," he said. "*You* are coming with me!"

Nathaniel wrenched free. "I cannot," he said. "And you must not accuse Mr. McInnis of kidnapping. I came here on my own."

He took another step back. How could he make his father understand? "I'm sorry, Father," he said, "but I cannot leave my home. The rice fields and marshes are all I know. And you taught me about them—you and Mother. Don't you remember?"

The room was quiet. Then Nathaniel's father slowly moved to an upholstered chair in the parlor and sat down heavily. The anger left his face. He looked old and tired. "I do remember our good times," he said. "But your mother is gone, and I'm so weary of fighting. I just want to go home—back to England."

"And I need to stay here," Nathaniel said. "It is my home."

His father sighed again. "Ah, Nathaniel. You are so like your mother. She loved this land, too."

He put out his hand. "Come here, lad. Don't be afraid. I'll not force you to leave." Nathaniel moved closer. His father put an arm around his shoulders. For the first time in a long time, it was a gentle touch.

"Will you watch over the boy?" Nathaniel's father asked

Mr. McInnis. "Perhaps he can claim the plantation someday."

Mr. McInnis nodded. "I'll watch both him and your plantation."

Nathaniel looked at his father. Suddenly, he was torn. If he stayed, he'd never see his father again—or Ben. His brother had slipped into the room.

"Don't stay, Nathaniel!" he said. "Come with us. Please."

For a moment, Nathaniel hesitated. Then he heard the whippoorwill again and felt the soft evening air. He thought of his mother's grave on the hill. This land was part of him, and he was part of it. He knew he couldn't leave.

"I'm sorry," he said, giving Ben a hug, "but I have to stay."

Nathaniel's father stood up. He squeezed Nathaniel's shoulder gently. "Keep your mother's gravesite well tended," he said.

Then he turned to Ben. "Come along. We'd best hurry if we're to get packed. The rebels will be arriving soon to take over the city."

Nathaniel stayed on the front porch long after they had left. When the sun began to rise over the rice fields, he could picture his father and Ben in a small boat, sailing east down the river to Tybee Island. There they would wait for British ships to take them back to England. But it was a new day in Savannah, and he would stay to build a new country.

Did you know . . . that the differences between Nathaniel and his father were not uncommon? During the Revolutionary War, neighbors, friends, and family members often found themselves on opposite sides. Even Benjamin Franklin, who helped write the Declaration of Independence, had a son, William, who was a Loyalist. William Franklin, who spent most of his childhood in England, served as royal governor of New Jersey from 1763 to 1776, when he was placed under house arrest by local patriots. Eventually, he was sent to Connecticut as a prisoner of war. In 1782, William returned to England. The differences between father and son caused a break in their relationship that never healed.

Do you wonder . . . what happened to the Loyalists, or Tories, after the Revolution? Between seventy-five thousand and one hundred thousand colonists, not all of them wealthy, remained loyal to Britain, and most of them left during or after the war. Those who could afford the trip returned to England. Thousands fled to Florida, which had remained loyal to Britain. Others were granted land in Canada, with about thirty-five thousand settling in Nova Scotia. But life was harsh in the cold climate of Canada, and those who returned to England were often disillusioned and homesick. Many continued to be Americans at heart, longing to return home. Thomas Hutchinson, the former royal governor of Massachusetts, wrote in his diary, "I would rather die in a little country farmhouse in New England than in the best nobleman's seat in Old England."

CONSTITUTION SUMMER

by Marcella Fisher Anderson

On September 3, 1783, the American Revolution ended formally when the United States, France, and Britain signed the Treaty of Paris. Yet the new country did not settle into peace and prosperity. Instead, turmoil and instability prevailed.

Much of this situation was due to the weaknesses of the Articles of Confederation, the document that formed a loose collection of independent states with no national executive and no judiciary. The states began to squabble among themselves, particularly over interstate commerce. Furthermore, without a strong central government to collect taxes, foreign debts could not be settled and back pay could not be provided for veterans.

A Continental army captain named Daniel Shays exemplified the Confederation's military weakness. In September of 1786, Shays led a veterans army of debt-ridden Massachusetts farmers against the courts that ordered foreclosures on farms and sentenced men to debtors prison. Then in January 1787, Shays and more than a thousand men advanced on the arsenal in Springfield, Massachusetts, to seize weapons. They were met and dispersed by the state militia. The Confederation government had no money to help Massachusetts. Marches and riots took place in other locations as well.

By spring, leaders of the new nation were acutely aware of the need for a stronger central government. A Constitutional Convention, composed of fifty-five delegates, was called in Philadelphia. Having reached a quorum by May 25, the gathering named George Washington president of the convention. Many of the delegates also had helped write the Declaration of Independence eleven years earlier. Notably missing were Thomas Jefferson and John Adams, who were abroad on official business—Jefferson in France and Adams in England. John Hancock, who had just been reelected governor of Massachusetts, decided to stay home to attend to state matters.

The convention opened on May 25. Within a few days, some of the delegates proposed writing a new constitution rather than revising the Articles of Confederation. A rule of secrecy was adopted on May 28. The delegates believed that public knowledge of sometimes bitter disagreements, such as those between northern and southern delegates, would only contribute to public unrest. Also, they wanted to feel free to change their minds on various issues without public censure.

Throughout the many long weeks of heated discussion, the delegates struggled to reach a consensus. While they debated behind locked doors and closed windows in the stifling heat, they were aware that history would judge them for their efforts, including their willingness to make compromises, their unwavering sense of purpose, and their clarity of vision. They were, after all, establishing a new country and writing the world's first national constitution.

IT HAD FINALLY RAINED. The week before, Philadelphia's cobblestone streets had glistened and water had dripped from the long iron pump handles on street corners. Yet now the gardens were dusty again, and the mulberry leaves drooped in the sun's heat.

Mary lifted her copies of the *Pennsylvania Gazette* for Wednesday, August 8, 1787. Under the sharp eyes of her employer, Mr. Sellers, she placed them in her leather pouch. Then she hitched up the outgrown pants she had borrowed from her brother, pulled down the brim of his old felt hat, and deepened her voice. "I'll go on my way now, sir," she said to Mr. Sellers. Imitating a boy's long strides as best she could, she made her way to the City Tavern through the early-morning sounds of dogs and roosters.

"The streets are crowded again," she said to the tavern keeper working on the front porch. "The delegates have returned from their recess."

The tavern keeper opened the door and pushed a wooden box of Madeira wine just inside. "Their work goes on and on—to what end, I do not know. All is secret."

"Indeed so. My brother Jonathan still stands guard at the State House door."

"You can set the newspapers inside today. It's a windy morning."

Before Mary could carry her papers to the table by the front entrance, three convention delegates banged through it and sat down in a booth. After ordering ale, they closed the curtains about them and started speaking quietly.

Mary caught only snatches of their conversation when the tavern keeper served them their drinks.

"I am overcome to see our decisions set down like this."

"In such orderly fashion. Yes, even to articles and sections."

"Every day we move closer to a new constitution."

A smile touched Mary's face. "They are making progress," she said to herself.

But before her thoughts could run on, she saw a tall, featureless figure standing in the doorway, his shape backlighted by the sun. His long hands dangled at his sides. He stood there a minute, a dark shadow, then entered and moved slowly to a table near the three men in the booth.

Mary watched him. He greeted the tavern keeper in a rude voice. Was he one of those who were still loyal to Britain?

She remembered what Jonathan had told her one evening: "There are people about who hope the delegates will fail in their efforts to write a constitution for our new nation. They watch for chances to undermine the work of the convention."

"But how?" Mary had asked.

"By twisting pieces of information dropped by loose tongues and passing on falsehoods to the newspapers. That's one way."

When Mary left the tavern to complete her deliveries, the man was still sitting at the table, listening carefully to the three men in the booth. Just outside, she saw a sheet of paper that had blown around the stems of a boxwood. She drew out the sheet and carried it into the sun, smoothing it as she read:

"Section 8. The Congress shall have Power to lay and collect Taxes. . . . To regulate Commerce with foreign Nations, and among the several States, and with the Indian Tribes."

Mary was reading so thoughtfully that she didn't notice that someone was looking over her shoulder. She gasped, knowing at once that the paper had been accidentally dropped by one of the delegates still in the tavern. As she turned around, she crashed into the stranger just behind her, striking his chest so hard that his silver buttons scratched her cheek. She stifled a cry when his strong hands seized the printed sheet from her fingers.

The man ran down a crowded lane. Mary gave chase, certain now that he was up to no good—one of those Jonathan had warned her about. She hid her heavy pouch of newspapers behind a bench and ran on, grateful that long skirts did not hamper her flying feet.

The man zigzagged in front of her and fumbled to pocket the paper. The streets were filled now with hawkers ringing their bells. Mary lost sight of him in the crowd.

At the top of Market Street, the Delaware River shone just below her. She stopped to catch her breath, taking in the view of ships' crews disembarking passengers and unloading barrels. The market stretched down to the water. Dogs and children ran among the covered stands set out with eggs, meat, pippin apples, fish, and piles of hard cheese.

Suddenly, she spied the man again, tall among the crowd. A farm cart loaded with cabbages and summer squash stood near her, its front wheels stopped by heavy bricks. She moved the bricks away, first one, then the other. Slowly, the cart started moving. It picked up speed as it neared the bottom of the hill.

The man stood there, his spectacles on, reading the sheet of paper. He moved to his right just as the wagon changed direction, too, making straight for him.

With cries of alarm, people scurried out of the way. Absorbed in his reading, the man did not hear the warnings. He looked up just as flying vegetables from the cart struck his chest and the cart crashed into him.

Mary hurried down the hill. She tugged at a corner of the important paper buried beneath the vegetables. It was wet with the juice of shattered squash but still legible. The people gathered around the accident did not notice her.

Carefully, she wiped the paper on her shirt. Trying not to attract attention, she walked slowly up the hill to the State House. Jonathan had just been relieved for half an hour. He stood in the yard under a small mulberry tree, his hat off. He wiped the sweat from his neck as Mary handed him the paper.

"Where did you get this?" he demanded sharply.

Mary could not suppress a smile. "I can't tell you now. I have newspapers to deliver."

Quickly, Jonathan folded the sheet into his uniform pocket. "I will give this to Mr. Madison when the session ends. We can talk later."

When Mary returned to the bench to retrieve her newspapers, the pouch was empty. A coldness touched her heart. She dragged up the stairs to Mr. Sellers's office. His mouth opened in surprise when he saw her. "You have delivered the newspapers already?"

"No, sir." She felt a flush move across her face.

"Why is that?"

"My copies of the *Gazette* were stolen, sir, save those for the City Tavern."

He set down his quill pen.

"I was inept, sir. I was detained by someone." That much was honest. She dared not tell him what had happened. She would appear disloyal for not bringing the document straight to him. It was the kind of news all Philadelphia waited for.

Mr. Sellers's eyes moved down to her feet, which she had forgotten to place sturdily apart. "Suppose you tell me your name again."

She swallowed once. "Mary, sir."

"Not Martin, as you first told me? And where did you get those clothes?"

"From my brother, sir. He's the one who urged me to come to Philadelphia to earn wages. Pretending to be a boy was the only way I could find work. Our father cannot pay his debts. My oldest brother has never been paid for his army service. He was wounded—he has but one arm now. We have lost our mill . . ." She bit down hard, drawing blood from her quivering lip.

Mr. Sellers shouted. "Unemployment, is it? Hard times, is it?" His face reddened. "This new country—America—is in chaos!" He thought for a long moment.

Finally, he said, "Very well, you may stay on as long as the convention still meets into early fall—and as long as no one finds you out. But you must pay a portion of your wages for the stolen newspapers. Do you understand?" He took in a deep breath and looked at her hard.

Carefully, he placed his quill pen in the pewter inkwell. "I am just a poor printer of a newspaper, Mary, but I study and think about everything I read. I believe the new constitution will do nothing to change the lives of women or slaves. It's a man's world—a free white man's world. Come September, you must go back where you belong. Home."

Home. Suddenly, the very word sounded good. It would be apple-picking time.

Later in the day, as Mary walked with Jonathan past Christ Church, she grasped his arm and said, "When I get home, I'm going to make a scarecrow with these clothes and set it up in Mama's corn patch. It will help me never to forget my summer here in Philadelphia." She smiled up at her brother. "As if I ever would."

Did you know . . . that a number of states, notably New York, called for changes in the Constitution? Several well-known citizens, including Thomas Jefferson, also did. Jefferson wrote letters from Paris urging the addition of a bill of rights. Their voices were heard. In 1791, ten amendments guaranteeing individual liberties were added to the Constitution.

Do you wonder . . . what some of the delegates said regarding the Constitution? Perhaps the most famous remark was made by Benjamin Franklin. Throughout the proceedings, Franklin observed a gilded carving of a half sun on the back of the chair where George Washington sat. During the signing of the Constitution on September 17, 1787, he commented to fellow delegates, "I have . . . often and often in the course of the Session . . . looked at that behind the President without being able to tell whether it was rising or setting: But now at length I have the happiness to know that it is a rising and not a setting Sun."

LEARNING FROM THE PRESIDENT

by J. W. Reese

After many long, often heated debates, the Constitutional Convention was ready to present the new Constitution to the states on September 17, 1787. The document begins, "We the People of the United States, in Order to form a more perfect Union, . . . do ordain and establish this Constitution for the United States of America."

Each state was to call a special convention to approve, or ratify, this plan for how the country should be governed. The delegates decided that ratification by nine out of the thirteen states would be enough to approve the new government.

Once the Constitution was ratified, the **Electoral College** *unanimously elected George Washington to be president of the new*

ELECTORAL COLLEGE—*A group of electors (people selected to cast a vote) who elect the president of the United States. When Americans go to the polls to vote for president, they are really voting for electors in their states who have pledged to vote for the people's candidate.* (For more information about the Electoral College, see the Glossary on page 137.)

United States of America. John Adams of Massachusetts, who came in second, became vice president. Washington was a reluctant president. Although he was flattered by the people's confidence in him, he would have preferred to remain at home in Virginia rather than assume such a great responsibility again. In the end, however, he agreed to accept the office.

He wrote in his diary on April 16, 1789, "I bade adieu to Mount Vernon, to private life, and to domestic felicity, and with a mind oppressed with more anxious and painful sensations than I have words to express, set out for New York."

As Washington rode to New York City, where the inauguration would take place, he was cheered all along the way. Everywhere, admiring citizens showed their gratitude for all he had done as leader of the Continental army. When he entered Pennsylvania, he was presented with a beautiful white horse and escorted into Philadelphia. After traveling through New Jersey, he boarded a barge to take him to Manhattan. As he crossed New York Harbor, cannon boomed a thirteen-gun salute. The barge landed at the foot of Wall Street, and Washington walked from there to his house on Cherry Street. Cheering crowds surrounded him.

Despite his great popularity, Washington was worried about the inauguration and the celebrations surrounding it. Americans might be offended if the inauguration reminded them of the coronation of a king. But if there wasn't enough ceremony, other countries might not respect the president of the new country. They had to strike a balance.

The citizens of New York had no such concerns. They were eager to welcome Washington and celebrate his election. Some might even have hoped to meet the great man. Imagine how nervous a young boy would have been if he had to make a speech and present a gift to the new president.

"I CAN'T DO IT," said Jeremy. "I just can't do it."

"But, Jeremy, you must give your speech and present the maple syrup to General Washington. You must," said Mother.

"But even thinking about it, I get so nervous I get the shakes. My knees tremble, and . . ."

Jeremy stopped. How could he make Mother understand? General Washington was forbidding enough, but tomorrow the general would be sworn into office as the first president of the new United States. He—Jeremy—would have to make a speech to the president.

"Jeremy!" Mother's voice was firm. "Our friends and neighbors are depending on you. You know they chose you to deliver the syrup because your father was Captain Gillet, Maple Hill's highest-ranking officer killed in the Revolution."

"I know." Jeremy slumped into a chair and gazed at the floor. "I promised to give the syrup as a gift from all our neighbors. But Mother, when we arrived here in New York City and I saw all those people, I got scared."

Mother twisted her hands. "You have your speech all memorized, do you not?"

"Of course. I could say it in my sleep," said Jeremy.

"Then just give the syrup to our new president, recite your speech, and it will all be over. If you can say it in your sleep, you won't forget it that easily."

"No, I know how it goes," said Jeremy. He rose to his feet and stood tall. "Mr. Washington, sir, on behalf of all the patriots of Maple Hill, West Stockbridge, Massachusetts, I . . ." He paused. "No, Mother, remembering the speech is not the problem."

A knock sounded. Mother opened the door and welcomed a man with a round red face and kind eyes. "Mr. Van Dong! Come in!"

Mr. Van Dong noticed Jeremy's unhappiness at once. "Young Gillet, why are you so sorrowful? Should you not be full of joy at seeing our new president tomorrow?" he asked.

"Jeremy does not feel that he can deliver the speech," said Mother.

"Why? Are you sick?" He placed his hand on Jeremy's forehead. "I do not feel any fever." He turned to Jeremy's mother. "Is it that the food here in New York does not agree? I came to invite you both downstairs for supper, but perhaps I should tell Frau Van Dong to make some good hot broth instead." He turned to the door.

"No, it's not that." Mother sighed. "Tell him, Jeremy."

Jeremy was reluctant to talk. He kept his head down and said, finally, in a low voice, "I'm just afraid of all the people here."

"Ah!" Mr. Van Dong said softly. "Full of fear, is it?" He stared at Jeremy. "Afraid of all the eyes on you?"

"Yes, sir."

"Afraid you will forget what it is you are to say?"

"No, sir. I can remember that all right," said Jeremy. "But my knees get weak even thinking about it, and I am afraid I may even . . ." He swallowed and then continued, "I may even drop the jug of maple syrup at the general's feet."

"Ah!" Mr. Van Dong sat down. "And how shall we help you, Master Jeremy, to feel more able to do what you must?"

Jeremy felt a small sense of relief. This great Dutch

merchant, in whose home they were staying, could surely think of something.

"You could, of course, send the jug and a note by messenger," said Mr. Van Dong. "But that would not satisfy your friends who sent you here. They could have done that themselves. Or you could have someone else hand the new president the jug while you recite the speech," he continued. "But that would not satisfy the wobbly knees, pale face, and moist hands, no?"

"No," said Jeremy.

Again the Dutchman was silent. Then came a loud "Ah!" Mr. Van Dong rose to his feet. "Much of fear is a sense of the unknown. Perhaps if you could see the great general beforehand, say at the inauguration itself, you would not be so frightened afterward, eh?"

Jeremy nodded, although secretly he doubted that even that would help.

"Space is very hard to obtain in Federal Hall. Only a few New Yorkers have seats. Even I must stand. But perhaps a small boy . . ."

Mr. Van Dong faced Jeremy's mother. "I can take Jeremy with me and make room for him. I have a little influence here. Then after the president's address, we can go to his house on Cherry Street. You and Mrs. Van Dong can meet us there. We will greet Mr. Washington when he returns from the service at St. Paul's Chapel, and Jeremy can present him with the maple syrup."

Mr. Van Dong walked to the door. "Come, Mrs. and Master Gillet. Let us partake of Frau Van Dong's fine cooking and then get a good night's rest for tomorrow.

April 30, 1789, will be a day we shall all remember, eh?"

Jeremy woke the next morning to the sound of church bells joyously ringing. By noon, he and Mr. Van Dong were pushing their way through the crowd on Wall Street. It seemed as if everyone in New York wanted to see General Washington being sworn in as president.

Once inside Federal Hall, Jeremy and Mr. Van Dong went to the Senate Chamber. It, too, was crowded, but they found an empty corner where they could stand.

Jeremy looked over the newly decorated chamber, the solemn senators and representatives dressed in their finest, and the great crowd of spectators. His gaze was carried to the ceiling, upon which were painted a sun and thirteen stars. Ahead of Jeremy were three windows. Beneath the middle window was a small platform with three empty chairs. A large door opened to an outside balcony.

"Look, Jeremy," said Mr. Van Dong, pointing to a short but distinguished-looking man standing across the room. "There is Mr. John Adams, the vice president."

Jeremy watched Mr. Adams join a small group of senators and representatives. All talked softly as they waited for Mr. Washington. The solemn men and the air of ceremony made Jeremy more aware of the enormity of what he must yet do. His fears returned in full force, but the heavy hand of the kind Dutchman resting on his shoulder reassured him.

After a long wait amid whispers and muted coughs, the great moment arrived. Vice President John Adams met General Washington at the door with the words, "Sir, the Senate and House of Representatives of the United States are ready to attend you to take the oath required by the Constitution, which will be administered to you by the chancellor of the State of New York."

"I am ready to proceed," replied the general.

Mr. Adams led General Washington through the room to the balcony outside. A loud roar came from the crowd waiting on Wall Street.

Jeremy could no longer see, but he could hear the general taking the oath of office: "I do solemnly swear that I will faithfully execute the office of the President of the United States, and will to the best of my ability, preserve, protect and defend the Constitution of the United States." Then the new president added, "So help me God."

Loud cheers came from the streets. The new republic had its first president! After a few minutes, President Washington came back inside the Senate Chamber to give his inaugural address. Jeremy gazed at the president's face. He seemed pale and anxious. *What's wrong?* Jeremy wondered. *Is he ill?*

"Fellow citizens of the Senate and of the House of Representatives," President Washington began. "Among the vicissitudes [difficulties] incident to life, no event could have filled me with greater anxieties."

The great man seemed nervous and uneasy. He moved his papers from one hand to the other, as if he couldn't decide where they belonged.

Could it be? wondered Jeremy. *Could it be that our president is nervous, too, after all he has been through during the Revolution?*

As President Washington continued, Jeremy was certain of it.

Why, if the greatest man in the world could do what he had to do in spite of the way he felt, Jeremy could certainly do the same. He would deliver his speech to the president on behalf of all the patriots of Maple Hill and present the jug of maple syrup. He would do it even if he was afraid.

And later that afternoon, that is just what he did.

The bells were still ringing when Jeremy, his mother, and the Van Dongs walked home. The joyful tolling seemed to match the ringing in Jeremy's heart.

"We don't know what the future will bring, do we, eh?" said Mr. Van Dong.

"No," replied Jeremy. "But we shall be of good courage."

Did you know . . . that George Washington was the only president elected unanimously? At that time, each elector cast two ballots. Washington was chosen by all the electors. John Adams, who received the second-highest number of votes, became vice president.

Do you wonder . . . why Washington's inauguration was held in New York City? Philadelphia, where the Declaration of Independence and Constitution were written, might seem to have been the logical choice. In 1789, however, New York was the capital of the new nation, and thus the first inauguration took place there.

George Washington

TIME LINE

1763 Britain wins French and Indian War.

1764 Parliament passes Sugar Act.

1765 Parliament passes Stamp Act.

1766 Parliament repeals Stamp Act but passes Declaratory Act, reasserting its right to tax the colonies.

1767 Parliament passes Townshend Acts, imposing new taxes on everyday household items. Some colonists riot in protest.

1768 British troops arrive in Boston to keep order.

1770 Parliament repeals most of the Townshend Acts but keeps the tax on tea.

British troops fire on a disorderly mob in Boston on March 5. Five colonists are killed, six wounded. This event becomes known as the Boston Massacre.

1773 Boston patriots protest the tea tax with the Boston Tea Party on December 16.

1774 First Continental Congress meets in Philadelphia.

1775 Paul Revere and others ride to warn the Massachusetts countryside that British troops are leaving Boston. Shots are fired at the Battles of

	Lexington and Concord on April 19.
	Second Continental Congress meets in Philadelphia in May. It establishes the Continental army, appoints George Washington commander in chief, and makes a last, failed effort to reconcile differences with Britain.
	Battle of Bunker (or Breed's) Hill on June 17 becomes the first major test of the colonial forces. They lose the battle, but at great cost to the British.
1776	Continental Congress continues to meet in Philadelphia.
	British army evacuates Boston on March 17. In August, the British occupy Long Island and New York City.
	Declaration of Independence is adopted on July 4.
	Washington and his army cross the Delaware River on Christmas night and attack Hessian forces quartered in Trenton, New Jersey. This victory gives a much-needed boost to the patriots.
1777	In Pennsylvania, Washington suffers defeat at the Battle of Brandywine, and Philadelphia falls to the British in September. The following month, the Continentals lose at Germantown.
	Continental army defeats the British at Saratoga, New York. British general John Burgoyne surrenders to American general Horatio Gates on October 17.
1777–1778	Continental army winters at Valley Forge, suffering from lack of food and warm clothing. Baron Friedrich von Steuben helps turn the soldiers into a well-trained army.
1778	France enters the Revolution on the side of the colonies.
	Britain seizes Savannah, Georgia, in December.
1780	Britain lays siege to Charleston, South Carolina. American general Benjamin Lincoln surrenders his army and the city on May 12.

Patriot forces defeat the Loyalist militia of British major Patrick Ferguson at Kings Mountain, South Carolina, on October 7.

1781 Patriot forces win the Battle of Cowpens, in South Carolina, on January 17.

Articles of Confederation are ratified to govern the new nation.

British general Charles Cornwallis brings his troops to Yorktown, Virginia. Washington's Continental army, aided by French troops and the French fleet, lays siege to Cornwallis and forces his surrender on October 19.

1782 Informal peace talks begin with Britain in April.

Americans regain control of Savannah in July and Charleston in December.

1783 Articles of Peace are signed on January 20; provisional treaty is ratified by Congress on April 15; final treaty is signed in Paris on September 3 by representatives of Britain, France, and the new United States.

1786 Internal uprisings exemplify the weakness of the federal government under the Articles of Confederation.

1787 Constitutional Convention begins meeting in Philadelphia on May 25 and presents the new Constitution to the states on September 17.

1788 Nine states ratify the Constitution by June 21, but the large states of New York and Virginia are needed. Virginia ratifies on June 25; New York ratifies on July 26.

1789 George Washington is inaugurated the first president of the United States on April 30.

1791 The states ratify the Bill of Rights, and it becomes part of the United States Constitution.

GLOSSARY

Electoral College—A group of electors (people selected to cast a vote) who elect the president of the United States. The Electoral College was originally established because the Founding Fathers didn't think the voters could make a good choice for president, especially since communication over great distances was difficult at the time. How, they reasoned, would a voter in Georgia evaluate a candidate from Massachusetts? They decided instead to have each state select a group of men to be electors and to have those electors choose the president and vice president. In some states, the state legislature selected the electors; in others, the voters did. As time went on, more states allowed for the direct election of the electors.

There have been changes in how the Electoral College works, but it is still used in choosing our president today. When Americans go to the polls to vote for the president, they are really voting for electors in their states who have pledged to vote for the people's choice. The number of electors each state has is determined by the number of members it has in the House of Representatives plus the number of senators (which is two for each state). The Constitution does not bind the electors to follow the vote of the people, but they almost never go against the popular vote. Some states have even made it illegal for electors to ignore the wishes of the voters. In almost all of the states, the candidate with the most votes receives all of that state's electoral votes.

ensign—In the British army, an ensign was a young commissioned officer who was often a teenager. He was assigned to carry the flag.

firecake—A simple, unleavened bread that many men in the Continental army at Valley Forge ate to keep from starving. It consisted of flour mixed with water and salt (if they had it) and was cooked on a griddle or stone.

guerrillas—Unofficial military groups operating in small bands to sabotage the enemy.

Hessians—German soldiers who were hired by the British to fight for them. Most of the Hessian victories came during the early fighting in New York State, but throughout the conflict they were generally feared by the Americans. The Hessian presence made Loyalists feel uneasy because they had expected to be entirely protected by British troops. During the war, the Continental Congress printed propaganda pamphlets written in German that encouraged the Hessians to desert the British. When the war ended, nearly five thousand Hessians settled in the new nation.

minutemen and militiamen—Citizen soldiers who trained to defend their villages and farms from any enemy. Service in the militia was a long tradition in New England, and most towns had a militia made up of all able-bodied men between the ages of sixteen and fifty. In 1774, with trouble brewing with Britain, the Provincial Congress suggested that some militiamen be organized into "minute companies" that could be ready to march on a minute's notice. These minutemen usually trained more often and more vigorously than other militiamen. Many towns had both a standing militia and minutemen.

Passover—A Jewish commemoration of the Exodus of the ancient Hebrews from enslavement in Egypt. It is celebrated by the Seder, a traditional dinner.

plantation—A large farm or estate on which crops are grown, often by workers who live on the plantation. In the colonial South, plantations were made possible by slave labor, which allowed one person or family to cultivate several hundred acres or more. Rice was the main crop in Savannah. By the beginning of the American Revolution, there were about fourteen hundred rice plantations in the area, with an average size of 850 acres.

redcoats—A name the colonists gave to the British regulars because of the red uniforms they wore. Another, more insulting name was lobsterbacks.

siege—The encirclement of an army or city by enemy forces. Starvation and/or bombardment are used to force those who are trapped to surrender.

Sons of Liberty—Patriot groups first organized to protest against British taxes in the 1760s. They began as secret societies, with membership known only to other members, but later worked to build popular support for their cause. Sometimes they resorted to mob actions and attacked Tories or British officials. They were the leaders of the Boston Tea Party.

Tories—Colonists who supported the British during the American Revolution. They were also called Loyalists.

FURTHER READING

Fiction

Collier, James Lincoln, and Christopher Collier. *My Brother Sam Is Dead.* Rev. ed. New York: Scholastic, 2003.

Denenberg, Barry. *The Journal of William Thomas Emerson: A Revolutionary War Patriot.* New York: Scholastic, 1998.

Edmonds, Walter D. *Drums Along the Mohawk.* Syracuse, N.Y.: Syracuse University Press, 1997.

Fast, Howard. *April Morning.* New York: Bantam/Domain, 1983.

Forbes, Esther. *Johnny Tremain.* Boston: Yearling, 1987.

Fritz, Jean. *Early Thunder.* New York: Viking, 1987.

Goodman, Joan. *Hope's Crossing.* Boston: Houghton Mifflin, 1998.

Gregory, Kristiana. *The Winter of Red Snow: The Revolutionary War Diary of Abigail Jane Stewart.* New York: Scholastic, 1996.

Lunn, Janet. *The Hollow Tree.* New York: Viking, 2000.

Massie, Elizabeth. *Son of Liberty.* New York: Tor, 2000.

Rinaldi, Ann. *Cast Two Shadows.* San Diego: Gulliver, 1998.

———. *The Fifth of March.* San Diego: Gulliver, 1993.

———. *The Secret of Sarah Revere.* San Diego: Gulliver, 2003.

———. *Time Enough for Drums.* New York: Laurel-Leaf Books, 2000.

———. *Wolf by the Ears.* New York: Scholastic, 1993.

Sterman, Betsy. *Saratoga Secret.* New York: Dial, 1998.

Wisler, G. Clifton. *Kings Mountain.* New York: HarperCollins, 2002.

Nonfiction

Adler, Jeanne Winston, ed. *In the Path of War: Children of the American Revolution Tell Their Stories.* Peterborough, N.H.: Cobblestone Publishing, 1998.

Fleming, Thomas. *Liberty! The American Revolution.* New York: Viking, 1997.

Hakim, Joy. *A History of US: From Colonies to Country, 1710–1791.* Book 3. New York: Oxford University Press, 1999.

Kelly, C. Brian. *Best Little Stories from the American Revolution.* Nashville: Cumberland House, 1999.

Martin, Joseph Plumb. *Yankee Doodle Boy: A Young Soldier's Adventures in the American Revolution Told by Himself.* Edited by George F. Scheer. New York: Holiday House, 1995.

Yoder, Carolyn P., ed. "Revolutionary Era" collection of *Cobblestone* magazines. Peterborough, N.H.: Cobblestone Publishing, 1994. (Five issues: *The Boston Massacre; British Loyalists in the Revolutionary Era; Celebrating Our Constitution; The Constitution of the United States; Patriotic Tales of the American Revolution.*)

Web Sites

The American Presidency: gi.grolier.com/presidents

America's Story: americaslibrary.gov

History Matters: historymatters.gmu.edu